Pearl Sydenstricker Buck was born in West Virginia and taken to China as an infant before the turn of the century. The daughter of Presbyterian missionaries, the family lived in a town in the interior instead of the traditional missionary compound. Buck grew up speaking Chinese as well as English, and received most of her education from her mother. She received an M.A. from Cornell, and taught English literature in several Chinese universities before she was forced to leave the country in 1932 because of the revolution.

She wrote fifty-three books and is the most widely translated American author to this day. She has been awarded the **Pulitzer Prize**, the **William Dean Howells Award**, and the **Nobel Prize for Literature**. *East Wind: West Wind* is her first novel written and published while she was living and teaching at the University of Nanking in the late 1920s. She died in 1973.

Only one, who like the author has lived all her life in China, yet being American still holds to western concepts of romantic love, marriage, and the scope of filial duty—only a lover of China, but no convert to her code of family and clan supremacy over the individual could have written this beautiful novel ... This is Mrs. Buck's first novel and a striking piece of work.
—*The New York Times*

A novel off the beaten path, and a very good novel, too. Mrs. Buck has written with fine simplicity and delicacy and charm. One would say an exquisite book ... —*New York Evening Post*

Mrs. Buck knows her China intuitively . . . She tells more of contemporary China than a year of newspaper headlines or a shelf of volumes by political minded experts, and tells it entertainingly.
—*Books*

Other Novels by Pearl S. Buck

Pearl S. Buck

EAST WIND:
WEST WIND

MOYER BELL | Wakefield, Rhode Island & London

Published by Moyer Bell
This Edition 1993
Copyright © 1930 by Pearl S. Buck.

this publication may be
y form or by any means
ing photocopying, record-
system, without permission
ymbolde Way, Wakefield,
at Russell Street, London

**LIBRARY OF CONGRESS
CATALOGING-IN-PUBLICATION DATA**

Buck, Pearl S. (Pearl Sydenstricker), 1892-1973.
East wind: west wind/Pearl S. Buck.

p. cm.

1. Marriage—China—Fiction. I. Title.

PS3503.U198E2   1993   93-13214
813'.52—dc20   CIP
ISBN 1-55921-086-9

Cover illustration: *Former Masters of Professions
and Arts*. Shanxi Provincial Museum

Printed in the United States of America
Distributed in North America by Publishers Group West, P.O.
Box 8843, Emeryville, CA 94662, 800-788-3123 (in California
510-658-3453), and in Europe by Gazelle Book Services Ltd.,
Falcon House, Queen Square, Lancaster LA1 1RN England.

ACKNOWLEDGMENT

The author extends her gratitude to the editors of *Asia Magazine* for permission to reprint the portions of this book which have appeared in their publication.

EAST WIND:
WEST WIND

PART ONE

A Chinese Woman Speaks

❋❋❋❋❋❋❋❋❋❋❋❋❋❋❋❋❋❋

I

THESE things I may tell you, My Sister. I could not speak thus even to one of my own people, for she could not understand the far countries where my husband lived for twelve years. Neither could I talk freely to one of the alien women who do not know my people and the manner of life we have had since the time of the ancient empire. But you? You have lived among us all your years. Although you belong to those other lands where my husband studied his western books, you will understand. I speak the truth. I have named you My Sister. I will tell you everything.

You know that for five hundred years my revered ancestors have lived in this age-old city of the Middle Kingdom. Not one of the august ones was modern; nor did he have a desire to change himself. They all lived in quietness and dignity, confident of their rectitude. Thus did my parents rear me in all the

[3]

honored traditions. I never dreamed I could wish to be different. Without thinking on the matter it seemed to me that as I was, so were all those who were really people. If I heard faintly, as from the distance outside the courtyard walls, of women not like myself, women who came and went freely like men, I did not consider them. I went, as I was taught, in the approved ways of my ancestors. Nothing from the outside ever touched me. I desired nothing. But now the day has come when I watch eagerly these strange creatures—these modern women— seeking how I may become like them. Not, My Sister, for my own sake, but for my husband's.

He does not find me fair! It is because he has crossed the Four Seas to the other and outer countries, and he has learned in those remote places to love new things and new ways.

My mother is a wise woman. When at the age of ten I ceased to be a child and became a maiden, she said to me these words,

"A woman before men should maintain a flower-like silence and should withdraw herself at the earliest moment that is possible without confusion."

I remembered what she said, therefore, when I stood before my husband. I bowed my head and placed my two hands before me. I answered him nothing when he spoke to me. But oh, I fear he finds my silence dull!

When I examine my mind for something to interest him, it is suddenly as barren as rice-fields after the harvest. When I am alone at my embroidery, I think of many delicately beautiful things to say to him. I will tell him how I love him. Not, you mind, in the brazen words copied from the rapacious West. But in hidden words like these,

"My lord, did you mark this day how the dawn began? It was as if the dull earth leaped to meet the sun. Darkness. Then a mighty lift of light like a burst of music! My dear lord, I am thy dull earth, waiting."

Or this, when he sails upon the Lotus Lake in the evening,

"What if the pale wan waters should never feel how the moon draws them? What if the wave

[5]

should never again be touched to life by its light? Oh, my lord, guard thyself, and return to me safely, lest I be that pale wan thing without thee!"

But when he comes in, wearing the strange foreign dress, I cannot speak these things. Can it be that I am married to a foreigner? His words are few and carelessly spoken, and his eyes slide too hastily over me, even though I wear my peach-colored satin and have pearls in my freshly bound hair.

This is my sorrow. I have been married a bare month, and I am not beautiful in his eyes.

Three days have I pondered now, My Sister. I must use cunning and seek for a way to turn my husband's eyes to me. Do I not come of many generations of women who found favor in the eyes of their lords? There have been none lacking in beauty for a hundred years save only one, and that one Kwei-mei in the age of Sung, who was pitted with smallpox at the age of three years. Yet it is written that even she had eyes like black jewels and a voice

which shook men's hearts like wind in the bamboos
in spring. Her husband held her so dear that though
he had six concubines suitable to his wealth and
rank, none of them did he love so well as he loved
her. And my ancestress, Yang Kwei-fei—she who
bore upon her wrist a white bird—held the very
empire in the scented palms of her hands, since the
emperor, the Son of Heaven, was mad with her
beauty. I, therefore, the least of these honorable
ones, must yet have their blood in my blood, and
their bones are my bones.

I have examined myself in my bronze mirror. It
is nothing for my sake but only for his when I tell
you I see that there are others less fair than I. I see
that my eyes are clearly defined, the white from the
black; I see that my ears are small and delicately
pressed to my head, so that the rings of jade and
gold cling close; I see that my mouth is small also,
and makes the approved curve in the oval of my
face. I wish only that I were not so pale, and that
the line of my brows were carried an eighth of an
inch further toward the temples. I correct my pale-

ness with a touch of rose upon my palms rubbed against my cheeks. A brush dipped in black perfects my brows.

I am fair enough then, and prepared for him. But the instant his eyes fall on me I perceive that he observes nothing, neither lips nor brows. His thoughts are wandering over the earth, over the sea, everywhere except where I stand waiting for him!

❊

When the geomancer had set the day for my marriage, when the red lacquered boxes were packed to the brim, when scarlet flowered satin quilts were heaped high on the tables, and the wedding cakes piled like pagodas, my mother bade me come to her room. I washed my hands and smoothed my hair freshly and entered her apartments. She had seated herself in her black carved chair and was sipping her tea. Her long, silver-bound bamboo pipe leaned against the wall beside her. I stood before her with my head drooping, not presuming to meet her eyes. Nevertheless I felt her keen gaze covering my face, my body, my feet. Its sharp warmth penetrated to

[8]

my very heart through the silence. At last she bade me sit. She toyed with watermelon seeds from a dish on the table beside her, her face quiet in its accustomed expression of inscrutable sadness. My mother was wise.

"Kwei-lan, my daughter," she said, "you are about to marry the man to whom you were betrothed before you were born. Your father and his were brother-friends. They swore to unite themselves through their children. Your betrothed was then six years of age. You were born within the circle of that year. Thus you were destined. You have been reared for this end.

"Through these seventeen years of your life I have had this hour of your marriage in mind. In everything I have taught you I have considered two persons, the mother of your husband and your husband. For her sake I have taught you how to prepare and to present tea to an elder; how to stand in an elder's presence; how to listen in silence while an elder speaks whether in praise or blame; in all things I have taught you to submit yourself as a flower submits to sun and rain alike.

[9]

"For your husband I have taught you how to decorate your person, how to speak to him with eyes and expression but without words, how to—but these things you will understand when the hour comes and you are alone with him.

"Therefore, you are well versed in all the duties of a gentlewoman. The preparation of sweetmeats and delicate foods you understand, so that you may tempt your husband's appetite and set his thoughts upon your value. Never cease to beguile him with your ingenuity in different dishes.

"The manners and etiquette of aristocratic life— how to enter and leave the presence of your superiors, how to speak to your inferiors, how to enter your sedan, how to greet his mother in the presence of others—these things you know. The behavior of a hostess, the subtlety of smiles, the art of hair decoration with jewels and flowers, the painting of your lips and fingernails, the use of scent upon your person, the cunning of shoes upon your little feet—ah, me, those feet of yours and all the tears they have cost! But I know of none so small in your generation. My own were scarcely more tiny at your age.

I only hope that the family of Li have paid heed to my messages and have bound as closely the feet of their daughter, the betrothed of your brother, my son. But I am fearful of it because I hear she is learned in the Four Books, and learning has never accompanied beauty in women. I must send word to the go-between again regarding the matter.

"As for you, my child, if my daughter-in-law equals you, I shall not complain over-much. You have been taught to play that ancient harp whose strings have been swept by generations of our women for the delight of their lords. Your fingers are skillful, and your nails are long. You have even been taught the most famous verses of the old poets, and you can sing them sweetly to your harp. I cannot see how even your mother-in-law will find anything lacking in my work. Unless you should bear no son! But I will go to the temple and present the goddess with a gift, should you pass the first year without conception."

My blood rose to my face. I cannot remember when I did not know of birth and motherhood. The desire for sons in a household like ours, where my father had three concubines whose sole interest was in the conceiving and bearing of children, was too ordinary to contain any mystery. Yet the thought of this for myself—but my mother did not even see my hot cheeks. She sat absorbed in meditation and fell to toying again with the watermelon seeds.

"There is only one thing," she said finally, "he has been abroad to foreign lands. He has even studied foreign medicines. I do not know—but enough! Time reveals all. You are dismissed."

❄❄❄❄❄❄❄❄❄❄❄❄❄❄❄❄❄❄

II

I COULD not remember when my mother had spoken so many words, My Sister. Indeed, she seldom spoke, except to correct or to command. This was right, for no one else in our women's apartments was equal to her, the First Lady, in position or native ability. You have seen my mother, My Sister? She is very thin, you remember, and her face seems carved from ivory for its pallor and its calm. I have heard it said that in her youth before she was wed, she possessed the great beauty of moth eyebrows and lips of the delicacy of the coral-colored buds of the quince tree. Even yet her face, fleshless though it is, preserves the clear oval of the paintings of the ancient women. As for her eyes, the Fourth Lady has a clever tongue, and she said of them once,

"The First Lady's eyes are sad jewels, black pearls, dying from over-much knowledge of sorrow."

Ah, my mother!

[13]

There was none like her in my childhood. She understood many things and moved with a habitual, quiet dignity which kept the concubines and their children all fearful in her presence. But the servants disliked while they admired her. I used to hear them grumbling because they could not so much as steal the fragments in the kitchen without her discerning the matter. Yet she never reproved them loudly as the concubines did when they were angry. When my mother saw that which did not please her, few words dropped from her lips; but those words were pointed with scorn, and they fell upon the guilty one like sharp ice upon the flesh.

To my brother and to me she was kind, but still formal and undemonstrative, as indeed was proper for one in her position in the family. Of her six children, four were taken in early childhood by the cruelty of the gods, and she therefore valued her only son, my brother. As long as she had given my father one living son he could have no legal ground for complaint against her.

She was, moreover, secretly very proud of her son for his own sake.

You have seen my brother? He is like my mother, thin of body, delicate-boned, tall and straight as a young bamboo tree. As little children we were ever together, and he it was who first taught me to brush the ink over the characters outlined in my primer. But he was a boy and I only a girl, and when he was nine and I six years of age, he was taken out of the women's apartments into those where my father lived. We seldom met then, for as he grew older he considered it shameful to visit among the women; and moreover, my mother did not encourage it.

I, of course, was never allowed in the courts where the men lived. When first they separated my brother from the women I crept once in the dusk of the evening to the round moon-gate that opened into the men's apartments; and leaning against the wall opposite it, I peered into the courts beyond, hoping to see my brother perhaps in the garden. But I saw only men-servants, hurrying to and fro with bowls of steaming food. When they opened the doors into my father's halls, shouts of laughter streamed out, and mingled with it was the thin high singing of a woman's voice. When the heavy doors shut there was only silence over the garden.

I stood for a long time listening for the laughter of the feasters, wondering wistfully if my brother were then in the midst of the gayety, when suddenly I felt my arm pulled sharply. It was Wang Da Ma, my mother's chief servant, and she cried,

"Now will I tell your mother if I see this again! Who has ever seen before such an immodest maid to go peeping at the men!"

I dared not speak more than a whispered excuse for shame.

"I sought my brother only."

But she answered firmly,

"Your brother now is also a man."

Therefore I seldom saw him again.

But I heard that he loved study and early became proficient in the Four Books and the Five Classics, so that my father at last heeded his beseeching and allowed him to go to a foreign school in Peking.

At the time of my marriage he was studying in the National University in Peking, and in his letters home he constantly asked to be allowed to go to America. At first my parents would not hear to such a thing, nor did my mother ever agree to it. But my father disliked trouble, and I could see that in the end my brother might prevail by importuning.

In the two vacations he spent at home before I went away, he spoke much of a book he called "science." My mother felt this to be unfortunate, for she could see no use for this western knowledge in the life of a Chinese gentleman. The last time he came home he wore the clothes of a foreigner, and my mother was much displeased. When he came into the room, somber and foreign-looking, my mother struck her stick on the floor and cried,

"What is this? What is this? Do not dare to present yourself to me in such an absurd costume!"

He was obliged therefore to put on his own clothes, although he was angry and delayed for two days until my father laughed at him and commanded him. My mother was right. In Chinese clothes my brother appeared stately and a scholar. With his legs exposed in the foreign dress, he resembled nothing seen or heard of in our family.

But even on those two visits he seldom talked with me. I know nothing of the books he loved, for I could not spare the time from the many things necessary to fit me for marriage to pursue further the classics.

Of his own marriage of course we never spoke. It would not have been fitting between a young man and woman. Only I knew through eavesdropping servants that he was rebellious against it and would not marry, although my mother had tried three times to set the wedding date. Each time he had persuaded my father to postpone the matter until he had had further study. And I knew of course that he was betrothed to the second daughter of the house of Li, a family well established in the city in wealth and position. Three generations previous to ours the head of the house of Li and the head of our house ruled as governors in adjoining counties in the same province.

Of course we had not seen his betrothed. The affair

had been arranged by my father before my brother was a year old. Therefore it would not have been proper for our families to have any coming and going before my brother's marriage took place. Indeed, nothing was even spoken concerning the betrothed except once when I heard Wang Da Ma gossiping to the other servants thus,

"It is a pity that the daughter of Li is three years older than our young lord. A husband should be superior even in age. But the family is old and rich and—" Then she saw me and fell silent to her work.

I could not understand why my brother refused to marry. The first concubine laughed when she heard of it and cried,

"In Peking it must be he has found a beautiful Manchu!"

But I did not believe my brother loved anything except his books.

I grew up therefore alone in the courtyards of the women.

❋

There were of course the children of the concubines; but I knew my mother considered them only as so many mouths to be fed when she gave out the daily rations of rice and oil and salt, and she paid them no attention beyond ordering the necessary yards of plain blue cotton cloth for their garments.

As for the concubines, they were at heart only ignorant women, always quarreling and mortally jealous of one another's place in the affections of my father. They had caught my father's fancy at first through a prettiness which faded like flowers plucked in spring, and my father's favor ceased when their brief beauty was gone. But they never seemed to be able to perceive that they were no longer beautiful, and for days before his coming they would busy themselves with furbishing up their jewels and gowns. My father gave them money on feast days and when he was lucky at his gambling, but they spent it foolishly on sweetmeats and on the wines they loved; and then having nothing before his coming they borrowed money of the servants to buy new shoes and hair ornaments. The servants were contemptuous when they saw the concubines had lost my father's favor, and drove hard bargains with them.

The eldest concubine, a fat, pudgy creature, whose tiny features were sunken in the mountains of her cheeks, was notable for nothing except her small and beautiful hands, in which she took the greatest pride. She washed them in oils and stained the palms rose-red, and the smooth, oval nails she painted vermilion. Then she scented them with a heavy magnolia perfume.

Sometimes my mother would weary of this woman's empty vanity and a little maliciously would bid her do some coarse washing or sewing. The fat Second Lady dared not disobey, but she whined and complained secretly to the other concubines that my mother was jealous of her and wished to spoil her beauty for my father. This she said, nursing her hands the while and examining them with the greatest care to see if the delicate skin were at all bruised or thickened. I could not bear to touch her hands; they were hot and soft and melted in one's grasp.

My father had long since ceased to care for this woman, but he gave her money when he came and spent a night in her apartment, lest she cry in a loud voice in the courts and tease him with her reproaches.

She had, moreover, two sons and thus was entitled to some attention.

Her sons were fat and exactly resembled their mother, and I do not bring them to mind except as eating and drinking continually. They ate fully at the table with the others, yet afterwards they would creep away into the servants' courtyard and quarrel with the servants for the left-over bits. They went about always with great cunning, fearing my mother, who hated above all else greed for food. She herself never ate more than a bowl of dry rice with a bit of salted fish or a thin slice of cold fowl and a sip of scented tea.

I do not remember more about the Second Lady except that she was always much afraid of dying. She ate many sweet oily sesame cakes and, when she fell ill, lay groaning in great terror. Then she would call in the Buddhist priests and promise her pearl hair ornaments to the temple if the gods would make her well. But when she was well again she continued to eat cakes and feigned to forget the promise.

The second concubine, the Third Lady, was a dim woman, who spoke seldom and took little interest in the family life. She had five children, all girls except the youngest; and this had weakened her spirit and made her disconsolate. For the girls she cared nothing. They were neglected and held little higher than the slaves we bought for service. She spent her time in a sunny corner of the courtyard nursing the son, a heavy, sallow child, three years old and still unable to talk or walk. He cried a great deal and was forever dragging at her long, flabby breasts.

The concubine I liked best was the third, a little dancing girl from Soochow. Her birth name was La-may, and she was as pretty as the la-may flower itself, which puts out its pale gold blossoms from leafless branches in early spring. She was like them, dainty and pale and golden. She used to put no paint on her cheeks as others did, but only an emphasis of black on her narrow eyebrows and a touch of vermilion on her lower lip. We saw very little of her at first, for my father was proud of her beauty and took her with him everywhere.

The last year before my marriage she had been at home, however, waiting for her son to be born. He was a lovely boy, chubby and handsome, and she took him and laid him in his father's arms. Thus she repaid what he had given her of jewels and affection.

Before the child's birth the Fourth Lady had been in a continual mood of high excitement and tinkling laughter. Everywhere she was praised for her beauty; and indeed, I have never seen a loveliness to surpass hers. She wore jade-green satins and black velvet, with jade in her exquisite ears, and she scorned us all a little in spite of her careless generosity with the cakes and sweetmeats given her at the feasts she attended nightly with my father. She seemed to eat almost nothing herself—a sesame cake in the morning, after my father had left her, and at noon half a bowl of rice with a bit of bamboo shoot or a thin slice of salted duck. She loved foreign wines and coaxed my father to buy her a pale yellow liquid with silver-pointed bubbles darting upward from the bottom. It made her laugh and become very talkative and her eyes sparkle like black crystals.

Then she amused my father exceedingly, and he would bid her dance and sing for him.

※

But when my father feasted, my mother sat in her own apartment reading the stately sayings of Confucius. As for me, when I was a young girl I often wondered at those feast nights and longed to peep, as I once had when I sought my brother, between the carved crevices of the moon-gate into the men's apartments. But my mother would never allow it, I knew, and I was ashamed to deceive her.

One night, however—I am filled with shame now at my unfilial disobedience!—I crept secretly through the blackness of a moonless summer night and gazed again through the gate and saw into my father's apartments. I do not know why I did it—I no longer thought of my brother. Some strange fullness of vague desire had made me restless throughout the long hot day, and when the night came, filled with warmth and dusk and the thick scent of lotus flowers, the quietness of our women's rooms seemed a thing dead of itself. My heart beat hard as I gazed.

The doors were flung wide and the light from a hundred lanterns streamed out into the hot, still air. Within I saw men sitting at square tables eating and drinking and servants hurrying back and forth with food. Behind each man's chair stood the vine-slender figure of a girl. But seated at my father's side, the only woman at the table, was La-may. I could see her quite clearly, her face smiling a little, shining like a wax-petaled flower, as it turned to my father. She said something in a low voice, scarcely moving her lips, and a roar of laughter went up from the men. Her smile was unchanged, slight, subtle, and she did not laugh.

This time my mother herself discovered me. She seldom left the house even to walk in the courts, but the heat of the night had driven her forth, and her sharp eyes discerned me immediately. She commanded me to retire at once to my room and following me there she slapped the palms of my hands sharply with her folded bamboo fan and asked me scornfully if I desired to see harlots at their work. I was ashamed and wept.

The next day she ordered opaque shell lattices to

be placed over the moon-gate, and I never looked through it again.

But my mother was none the less kind to the Fourth Lady. The servants praised her loudly for this forbearance, although I think the other concubines would have been glad to see her cruel, as a first lady so often is to the others. Perhaps my mother knew what was in store.

After her baby was born, the Fourth Lady thought that of course my father would take her about with him again. She did not nurse the child herself lest she spoil her beauty. Instead she gave him to a sturdy slave-woman, whose child, a girl, had of course not been allowed to live. This slave was a thick-bodied woman with a foul mouth, but the little boy slept in her bosom all night, next her flesh, and was carried in her arms all day. His own mother paid little attention to him, except to dress him in red on a gala day and put little cat-faced shoes upon his feet and play with him a brief while. When he cried, she thrust him impatiently back into the slave's arms.

But the boy gave her an insufficient hold upon my father. Though legally she had repaid him, she

EAST WIND: WEST WIND

had daily to seek cunning devices to capture his senses, as our women have ever had to do. Even her cunning, however, was not enough. She was not so beautiful as she had been before the child's birth. Her smooth, pearly little face sagged just enough to take away her delicate youth. She dressed herself in her jade-green gown and hung pendants in her ears and gave her little tinkling laugh. My father appeared as pleased with her as ever; only, when he went on his next journey he did not take her with him.

Her astonishment and rage were dreadful to see. The other concubines were secretly pleased and smiled a great deal as they pretended to comfort her. My mother was a little kinder to her than usual. I heard Wang Da Ma mutter angrily,

"Oh, yes, now we shall soon have another idle woman to feed. He is weary of this one already!"

From that day the Fourth Lady brooded. She became discontented, with fits of irritability and profound weariness of the humdrum existence in a women's courtyard. She had been used to the feasting and the admiration of men. She became very melancholy, and later even tried to throw away her own life. But that was after my marriage. It is not to be supposed from all this that our life at home was a sad one. It was really very happy, and many of our neighbors envied my mother. My father had never ceased to respect her for her intellect and for her capable management of his affairs. She never reproached him for anything.

Thus they lived in dignity and peace.

O my beloved home! My childhood passes before me in pictures illumined as by firelight. The courtyards, where I watched the lotus-buds burst into flower in the pool at dawn, and the peonies bloom in their terraces; the family rooms, where the children tumbled on the tiled floor, and the candles flared before the house-gods; my mother's room, where I see her stern, delicate profile bent over a book, the huge canopied bed in the background.

Most dear of all is the stately guest-hall, with its

ponderous black teak couches and chairs, the long carved table and the scarlet satin curtains in the doorways. Above the table hangs a painting of the first Ming emperor—an indomitable face with a chin like a stone cliff—and on each side of this painting hang the narrow scrolls of gold. The whole south side of the hall is in carved window frames, latticed with rice-paper. This paper sheds a soft moonstone light over the dark dignity of the room, reaching even to the heavy beams of the ceiling and lighting up the vermilion and the gold of their painted edges. To sit quietly in this hall of my ancestors and watch the twilight fall upon it in dusky silence has ever been to me like music.

On the second day of the New Year, which is the day for great ladies to call upon one another, the hall is delicately gay. Into its dim age comes a host of brilliantly dressed ladies; there is light and laughter and bits of formal talk, and the slaves pass tiny cakes in red lacquered sweetmeat trays. My mother presides over it all with grave courtesy. The old beams have looked down upon the same scene for hundreds of years—black heads and dark eyes, rainbow silks and satins, jade and pearl and ruby hair ornaments, and turquoise and gold flashing upon slender ivory hands.

O my beloved home—O dearly beloved!

I see myself, a little solemn figure clinging to my brother's hand, standing beside the fire in the court, where the kitchen-gods are about to be burned. They have had honey put on their paper lips so that they may ascend to heaven with sweet words and forget thus to tell of the times when the servants quarreled, and when they stole food from the bowls. We are filled with awe at the thought of the messengers to the distant unknown. We do not speak.

I see myself on the Dragon Festival, with my best feast-day gown of pink silk embroidered with plum blossoms, scarce able to wait until evening when my brother will take me to see the dragon boat upon the river.

I see the bobbing lotus lantern that my old nurse brings me at the Feast of Lanterns, laughing at my excitement when night comes and I may light the smoky red candle within.

I see myself walking slowly beside my mother into

the great temple. I watch her place the incense in the urn. I kneel reverently with her before the god, and fear is cold within me.

✻

I ask you, My Sister, with years like this to shape me, how have I been prepared for such a man as my husband? All my accomplishments are of no avail. I plan in secret that I will wear the blue silk coat with black buttons cunningly wrought in silver. I will place jasmine in my hair, and upon my feet the pointed black satin shoes embroidered in blue. I will greet him when he enters. But when it has all come to pass, his eyes escape hastily to other things—his letters upon the table, his book. I am forgotten.

Within my heart is a writhing fear. I remember a day before my marriage. It was the day on which my mother wrote two letters swiftly with her own hand, one to my father and one to my future mother-in-law, and dispatched them in great haste by the old gate-keeper. I had never seen her so perturbed. On that day I heard the servants whisper that my betrothed wished to break our engagement because I was uneducated and had bound feet. I burst into tears, and the servants were frightened and swore that it was not I of whom they spoke, but of Lady Tao's fat second daughter.

Now I remember this and ponder it in great agitation. Could it have been I? Servants are ever liars! Yet I am not untaught. I have been carefully trained in all household matters and in the care of my person. As for my feet, surely no one could prefer huge, coarse ones like those of a farmer's daughter. It was not I—it cannot be I—of whom they spoke!

III

WHEN I had said farewell to my mother's home and stepped into the great red chair to be carried to the home of my husband, I never dreamed I should not please him. For myself, I remembered and was glad that I am small and lightly framed, with an oval face that others are pleased to look upon. At least here he would not be disappointed.

During the wine ceremony I stole a glance at him from under the red silken strands of my veil. I saw him standing there in his stiff, black, foreign clothes. He was tall and straight like a young bamboo. My heart went cold and hot together. I was sick for his secret glance. But he did not turn his eyes to pierce my veil. We drank the cups of wine together. We bowed before his ancestral tablets. I knelt with him before his august parents. I became their daughter, leaving forever my own family and clan. He never looked at me.

❄

That night, after the feasting and bantering laughter had ended, I sat alone upon the couch in the bridal chamber. I was stifled with my fear. The hour I had imagined and dreaded and longed for all my life was come—the hour when for the first time my husband looked on my face, and we were alone together. My cold hands were pressed against each other in my lap. Then he came in, still so tall and somber in those dark foreign clothes. He came to me at once, and in silence he lifted the veil from my face and looked long upon me. Thus he acknowledged me. Then he took one of my cold hands. The wisdom of my mother had taught me thus:

"Be chill, rather than warm. Be the tang of wine rather than the surfeiting sweetness of honey. Then his desire will never fail."

Therefore I was reluctant to give him my hand. Instantly he withdrew his own and gazed at me in silence. Then he began to speak with grave earnestness. At first I could not comprehend his words for the marvel of his voice in my ears, a quiet, deep man's voice that made my body flush with shyness. Then I caught his words with astonishment. What was he saying?

"It is not to be supposed that you would be drawn to me whom you behold for the first time, as I behold you also. You have been forced into this marriage as much as I have. We have been helpless in this matter until now. Yet now that we are alone we may create our life according to our own desires. For myself, I wish to follow the new ways. I wish to regard you in all things as my equal. I shall never force you to anything. You are not my possession—my chattel. You may be my friend, if you will."

These were the words I heard on my bridal night. At first I was amazed beyond understanding of their meaning. I equal to him? But why? Was I not his wife? If he did not tell me what to do, then who would? Was he not my master by law? No one had forced me to marry him—what else could I do if I did not marry? And how could I marry except as my parents arranged it? Whom could I marry if not

the man to whom I had been betrothed all my life?
It was all according to our custom. I did not see
wherein lay any force.

Then his words burned again in my ears. "You
have been forced into this as much as I have." I was
suddenly faint with fear. Did he mean to say he did
not wish to be married to me?

O My Sister, such anguish—such bitter pain!

I began to twist my hands in my lap, not daring to
speak, not knowing how to reply. He placed one of
his hands over both of mine, and we were silent for
a while. But I only wished that he would take his
hand away. I felt his eyes on my face. At last he
spoke, his voice low and bitter,

"It is as I feared. You will not—cannot—show me
your real mind. You dare not break away from what
you have been taught you should say and do at this
time. Listen to me—I do not ask you to speak. But
I beg of you this small token. If you are willing to
try the new path with me, bend your head a little
lower."

He watched me closely; I could feel his hand
pressing down steadily. What did he mean? Why

could not things proceed in the expected way? I was ready to be his wife. I desired to be the mother of sons. Oh, then my sorrow began—this heaviness that never leaves me by day or night! I knew not what to do. And in my despair and ignorance I bent my head.

"I am grateful," he said, rising to his feet and removing his hand. "Rest quietly in this chamber. Remember you will have nothing to fear, now or ever. Be at peace. I will sleep this night in the little chamber adjoining."

He turned swiftly and went away.

❄

O Kwan-yin, Goddess of Mercy, pity me—pity me! Such a child—so young, so terrified in my loneliness! Never had I slept away from my home before. Now to lie in solitude, knowing at last that I found no favor in his eyes!

I ran to the door, thinking in my wildness that I might escape and return to my mother's home. But my hand upon the heavy iron bar recalled me. For me there could never be any return. Even though by miracle I escaped through the unknown courtyards of my new home, there was the strange street; even though by miracle I found my way to the familiar gate, it would never open to receive me. If my voice moved the old gateman so that he allowed me to stumble through the doors of my childhood, my mother would be there waiting to send me back to my duty. I could see her, inexorable, sorrowful, commanding my instant return to my husband's house. I no longer belonged to her family.

I took off the wedding garment slowly then and folded it away. I sat for a long time on the edge of the great curtained bed, fearing to creep into the shadows within. His words tumbled madly about in my mind without meaning. At last tears rushed to my eyes, and I huddled under the coverings and sobbed for weary hours until a restless sleep fell lightly upon me.

At dawn I waked, at first in wonder as I saw the strange room, and then with a rush of miserable memory. I arose hastily and dressed myself. When the servant came in with the hot water, she smiled and glanced inquiringly about. I drew myself straight. I was glad I had learned dignity of my mother. At least no one should know that I had not pleased my husband. I said,

"Take the water to your master. He robes himself in the inner chamber."

I clothed myself proudly in brocade of crimson, and I hung gold in my ears.

A moon of days has passed since we met, My Sister! My life is confused with strange events.

We have moved away from his ancestral home! He dared to say that his honored mother was autocratic and that he would not have his wife a servant in the home.

It all came from a small matter indeed. When the wedding festivities were over, I presented myself to his mother thus: I rose early and, calling a slave, I desired her to bring hot water and I poured it into a brass basin and then, the slave proceeding before me, I went into the presence of my husband's mother. Bowing, I said to her,

"I beg that the honorable one will consent to refresh herself with bathing in this hot water."

She lay in her bed, a huge, mountainous mass under the satin quilts. I dared not look at her as she sat up to lave her hands and face. When she had finished she motioned me without speaking to remove the basin and withdraw. I do not know whether my hand caught in the heavy silken curtains of the bed, or whether—being frightened—my hand shook, so that when I lifted the basin it tipped, and a little water spilled upon the bed. I felt my blood stop with fright. My mother-in-law cried angrily in a hoarse voice,

"Now then! What is this for a daughter-in-law!"

I knew I must not speak to excuse myself. I turned therefore and bearing the basin unsteadily because of tears blinding my eyes, I went out from her presence. When I stepped from the door my husband was there, passing by, and I saw that for some reason he was angry. I feared that he would blame me because on the first occasion I did not please his mother. I could not lift my hands to wipe my tears off, and I felt them gather and break and run down my cheeks. I murmured foolishly like a child,

"The basin was slippery—"

But he interrupted me.

"I do not blame you. But I will have no more of this servant's work for my wife. My mother has a hundred slaves!"

I tried to tell him then that I wished to give his mother the proper obedience. My mother has instructed me carefully in all those attentions due from a daughter-in-law to the mother of her husband. I rise politely and remain standing in her presence. I lead her to the most honorable seat. I rinse her tea-bowl and pour slowly the freshly infused green tea and present it carefully with both hands. I may refuse her nothing. I must cherish her as my own mother, and her reproaches, however unjust, I must bear in silence. I am prepared to subject myself to her in all things. But his determination was fixed. He heeded nothing I said.

It is not to be supposed that the change was accomplished easily. His parents even commanded him to remain, according to the ancient custom, within the ancestral home. His father is a scholar, small and slight and stooped with learning. Sitting at the right of the table in the living hall, under the ancestral tablets, he stroked his spare, white beard three times and said,

"My son, remain in my house. What is mine is yours. Here is plenty of food and space. You need never waste your body in physical labor. Spend your days in dignified leisure and in study that suits your pleasure. Allow that one, the daughter-in-law of your honored mother, to produce sons. Three generations of men under one roof is a sight pleasing to Heaven."

But my husband is quick and impatient. Without stopping to bow to his father he cried,

"But I wish to work, my father! I am trained in a scientific profession—the noblest in the western world. As for sons, they are not my first desire. I wish to produce the fruit of my brain for my country's good. A mere dog may fill the earth with the fruit of his body!"

I, myself, peeping through the blue curtains at the door, heard the son speak thus to the father, and I was filled with horror. Had he been the eldest son, or had he been reared in the old ways, he could never have resisted his father thus. The years away in those countries, where the young do not revere the aged, have made him unfilial. True, he has spoken courteous words in parting to his parents; he has promised them that he has the heart of a son to them forever. Nevertheless, we have moved!

This new house is like nothing I have ever seen. It has no courtyard. There is only a tiny square hall from which the other rooms open, and from which a stair rises swiftly up. The first time I climbed this stair I was afraid to come down again, because of the steepness to which my feet are not accustomed. I sat down, therefore, and slipped from step to step, clinging to the wooden rail. I saw afterwards that a little of the fresh paint had come off upon my coat, and I hastened to change, lest my husband should ask about it and laugh at my fear. He laughs quickly and suddenly with a loud noise. I am afraid of his laughter.

As for the arranging of the furniture, I did not know how to place it in such a house. There was no room for anything. I had brought as part of my dowry from my mother's house a table and chairs of massive teak wood and a bed as large as my mother's marriage bed. My husband placed the table and chairs in a secondary room he calls "dining room," and the great bed I had thought would be the birth place of my sons cannot even be put up in any of the small upper rooms. I sleep upon a bamboo bed like a servant's, and as for my husband, he sleeps upon an iron bed as narrow as a bench and in another room. I cannot become accustomed to so much strangeness.

In the main room, or what he calls "parlor," he placed chairs he bought himself; curious, misshapen things they are, no one like the others, and some are even made of common reeds. In the center of this room he placed a small table and upon it, a cloth of pongee silk, and then some books. Ugly!

On the walls he hung framed photographs of his schoolmates and a square piece of felt cloth with foreign letters on it. I asked him if this were his diploma, and he laughed very much. He showed me

[45]

his diploma then. It is a piece of stretched skin inscribed with strange black characters. He pointed out his name with crooked marks after it. The first two signified his big college, and the second two his ability as a doctor in western medicine. I asked if these marks were equal in degree to our ancient "han-lin," and he laughed again and said there was no comparison. This diploma is framed behind glass and hangs in the honored place upon the wall, where, in the guest hall at my mother's house, is the stately painting of the old Ming emperor.

But this hideous western house! How, I thought, shall I ever feel it my home? The windows have large panes of clear glass instead of latticed carving with opaque rice paper. The hard sunlight glitters upon the white walls and startles each bit of dust upon the furniture. I am not accustomed to this merciless light. If I touch vermilion to my lips and smooth rice powder upon my brow as I have been taught to do, this light searches it out so that my husband says,

"Do not, I beg, paint yourself for me in this way. I prefer women to appear natural."

Yet not to use the softness of powder and the warmth of vermilion is to leave unfinished the emphasis of beauty. It is as though I should consider my hair brushed without the final smoothness of oil, or should place upon my feet shoes that had no embroidery. In a Chinese house the light is dimmed by lattice and carving and falls gently therefore upon the faces of women. How am I to be fair in his eyes in a house like this?

Moreover, these windows are foolish. My husband bought white cloth and told me to make curtains, and I marveled that first a hole is made in the wall and then glass set in and then that glass hung over with cloth!

As for the floors, they are of wood, and at every step my husband's foreign shoes clattered back and forth. Then he bought some heavy flowered woolen material and placed it on the floors in large squares. This astounded me very much. I was afraid we should soil it or that the servants would forget and spit upon it. But he was most indignant when I mentioned this, and he said we would have no spitting on the floor.

"Where then, if not on the floors?" I asked.

"Outside, if it must be done," he replied briefly.

But it was very difficult for the servants, and even I forgot sometimes and spat the shells of watermelon seeds upon the cloth. Then he bought small squat jars for every room and compelled us to use them. Strange, he himself uses a handkerchief, returning it to his pocket, even. A filthy western habit!

IV

AI-YA, there are hours when I would flee away if I could find the means! But I dare not return to my mother's face under such circumstances, and there is nowhere else to go. The days drag past, one after the other—long lonely days. For he works as though he were a laborer who must earn what rice he eats, instead of being what he is, the son of a wealthy official. Early in the morning, before the sun has even gathered the warmth of the fullness of day, he is gone to his work, and I am left alone until evening in this house. There are only the strange servants in the kitchen, and I am ashamed to listen to their gossip.

Ah me, I think sometimes it would be better to serve his mother and live in the courts with my sisters-in-law! At least I should hear voices and laughter. Here silence hangs over this house all day like a mist.

I can only sit and think and dream how to seize hold of his heart!

In the morning I rise early to prepare myself to appear before him. Even though I have not slept for restlessness in the night I rise early and wash my face in steaming, scented water and smooth it with oils and perfumes, longing to catch his heart unaware in the morning. But however early I rise, he is always at his table studying.

Each day it is the same. I cough softly and turn ever so slightly the round handle of his door.—Ah, those strange hard knobs, how I have had to turn and turn many times to learn their secret! He is impatient with my fumbling, and I practice therefore in his absence. But even then sometimes in the early morning my fingers slip upon the smooth, cold porcelain, and then my heart sinks as I try to make haste. He dislikes slowness and he moves his body so rapidly when he walks that I am afraid he will injure himself.

But he does nothing to protect his body. Day after day when I present the hot tea in the chill of the morning he accepts it without lifting his eyes from the book. Of what use is it then that I sent a servant at dawn to buy fresh jasmine for my hair? Even its fragrance does not creep through the pages of the foreign book. Eleven mornings out of twelve when I return in his absence to see if he has drunk his tea, he has not moved the lid from the bowl and the leaves float undisturbed in the pale liquid. He cares for nothing except his books.

I have pondered everything that my mother taught me concerning my husband's pleasure. I have prepared savory food to beguile his palate. I sent a servant, and he bought chicken freshly killed and bamboo shoots from Hangchow and mandarin fish and ginger and brown sugar and the sauce of soybeans. All morning I prepared the dishes, forgetting nothing that I had been told would increase the fullness and delicacy of flavor. When all was prepared I directed that the dishes should be brought in at the end of the meal that he might exclaim,

"Ah, the best has been kept until the last. It is food for an emperor!"

But when the dishes came he took them as part of the meal without question. He scarcely tasted them and made no speech of them. I sat watching him eagerly but he said nothing, eating the bamboo shoots as though they were cabbage from a farmer's garden!

That night when the pangs of my disappointment were past, I said to myself,

"It is because it is not his favorite dish. Since he never speaks his preference I will send to his mother and inquire what he liked in his youth."

I sent a servant therefore but his mother answered,

"Before he crossed the four seas, he loved duck's flesh roasted brown and dipped in the jellied juice of wild haws. But since his many years of feeding upon the barbarous and half-cooked fare of the western peoples, he has lost his taste and cares no more for delicate foods."

I tried no longer, therefore. There is nothing that my husband desires of me. He has no need of anything I can give him.

One evening after a fortnight in the new house we sat together in the parlor. He was reading one

of his large books when I entered, and I glanced at
the picture on the page as I passed to my seat and
saw that it was an upright human form but, to my
horror, without the skin—only the bloody flesh! I
was shocked and wondered that he read such things,
but I dared not ask him about it.

I sat there in one of the queer reed chairs, not leaning back because it seemed undignified to recline
thus in public. I was weary for my mother's home
and recalled that at this hour they would be gathering at supper, the concubines and their clamoring
little children, in the flaring candle light. My mother
is there in her place at the head of the table, and the
servants under her direction are placing the bowls
of vegetables and steaming rice and scattering chopsticks for all. Everybody is busy and happy over the
food. My father will come in after the meal and play
a bit with the concubines' children, and after the
work is done the servants will sit on tiny stools in
the courtyard, whispering together in the dusk. My
mother takes accounts with the head cook at the
dining table, a tall red candle sputtering its fitful
light upon her.

Oh, I was sick to be there! I would walk about among the flowers and examine the lotus-pods to see if the seeds were ripe within. It was late summer and nearly time for them. Perhaps, as the moon rose, my mother would bid me fetch my harp to play the music she loves; the right hand singing the air, and the left hand drifting into a minor accompaniment.

At the thought I rose to get my instrument. I removed it carefully from the lacquered case, upon which, inlaid in mother-of-pearl, are the figures of the eight spirits of music. Within, upon the harp itself, various woods are fitted together beneath the strings, each bit of wood adding its own note of richness when the strings are swept. The harp and its case had belonged to my father's mother and had been brought from Kwangtung for her by her father when she had ceased to weep at the binding of her feet.

I touched the strings softly. They gave out a thin and melancholy sound. This harp is the ancient harp of my people, and it should be played under the trees in the moonlight beside still water. There it gives out a sweet and faërie voice. But in this silent, foreign

[54]

room it was stifled and weak. I hesitated—then played a little song of the time of Sung.

My husband looked up.

"That is very nice," he said kindly. "I am glad you can play it. I will buy you a piano some day and you can learn to play western music, too." He turned back to his reading.

I looked at him as he read the ghastly book, and continued to touch the strings very softly without knowing what they sang. I had never even seen a piano. What would I do with the foreign thing? Then suddenly I could play no more. I put the harp away and sat with drooping head and idle hands.

After a long silence my husband closed his book and looked at me thoughtfully.

"Kwei-lan," he said.

My heart leaped. It was the first time he had called me by my name. What had he to say to me at last? I lifted my eyes timidly to him. He continued,

"I have wished ever since our marriage to ask you if you will not unbind your feet. It is unhealthful for your whole body. See, your bones look like this."

He took a pencil and sketched hastily upon the leaf of his book a dreadful, bare, cramped foot.

How did he know? I had never dressed my feet in his presence. We Chinese women never expose our feet to the sight of others. Even at night we wear stockings of white cloth.

"How do you know?" I gasped.

"Because I am a doctor trained in the West," he replied. "And then, I wish you to unbind them because they are not beautiful. Besides, foot-binding is no longer in fashion. Does that move you?" He smiled slightly and looked at me not unkindly.

But I drew my feet hastily under my chair. I was stricken at his words. Not beautiful? I had always been proud of my tiny feet! All during my childhood my mother herself had superintended the soaking in hot water and the wrapping of the bandages —tight and more tight each day. When I wept in anguish she bid me remember that some day my husband would praise the beauty of my feet.

I bowed my head to hide my tears. I thought of all those restless nights and the days when I could not eat and had no desire to play—when I sat on the edge of my bed and let my poor feet swing to ease them of their weight of blood. And now after enduring until the pain had ceased for only a short year, to know he thought them ugly!

"I cannot," I said, choking as I rose, and, unable to keep back my weeping, I left the room.

It was not that I cared over-much about my feet. But if even my feet in their cunningly embroidered shoes did not find favor in his sight, how could I hope to win his love?

Two weeks later I left for my first visit to my mother's home, according to our Chinese custom. My husband had not spoken of unbinding my feet again. Neither had he again addressed me by my name.

V

You weary not, My Sister? I will proceed, then!

Although I had been away so short a time, it seemed when I entered the familiar gate that a hundred moons had waned since I passed through in my bridal chair. I had hoped not a little then, and feared much. Now, although I came back a married woman, with my braid wrapped into a coil and my forehead bare of its girlhood fringe, still I knew that, after all, I was the same girl, only more afraid and more lonely and far less hopeful.

My mother came to the first courtyard to meet me, leaning on her long bamboo and silver pipe. She looked tired, I thought, and a little more worn than before; or perhaps it was only because I had not seen her daily. At any rate the added touch of sadness in her eyes drew me to her, so that, after bowing to her, I ventured even to take her hand. She responded with a light pressure and together we walked back to the family courtyard.

Oh, how eagerly I gazed at everything! It seemed that somehow there must be a great change. But everything was its natural self, ordered and quiet and accustomed in the courtyards, except for the laughter of the concubines' children and the bustling of busy servants, smiling and shouting in greeting as they saw me. The sunshine of early autumn streamed across the flower walls and glazed tiles in the courts, and shone upon the shrubs and pools. The latticed doors and windows on the south side of the rooms were thrown wide to catch the warmth and light, and the sun, filtering through, caught the edge of carven wood and painted beams within. Although I knew my place was no longer there, my spirit in spite of this rested in its true home.

I missed only one thing, one fair, teasing face.

"Where is the Fourth Lady?" I asked.

My mother called a slave to fill her pipe and then answered casually,

"La-may? Ah, I sent her to visit in the country for a change of air."

From her tone I knew better than to question further. But afterwards in the evening when I was preparing for sleep in my childhood room, old Wang Da Ma came in to brush out my hair and braid it as she always used to do. Then in her gossip of many things she told me that my father was thinking of taking a new concubine, a Peking girl who had been educated in Japan, and the Fourth Lady, when she heard of it, had swallowed her best jade earrings. She told no one for two days, though she suffered greatly, and then my mother discovered it.

The girl was at the point of death, and the old doctor who was called in could do nothing, although he pierced her wrists and ankles with needles. A neighbor suggested the foreign hospital, but my mother did not consider such a thing a possibility. We knew nothing of foreigners. Besides, how could a foreigner know what was wrong with a Chinese? Foreign doctors may understand the diseases of their own people, who are quite simple and barbarous in comparison with the highly complex and cultivated Chinese. My brother, however, happened to be at home just then for the Eighth Moon Festival, and he himself asked the foreign woman doctor to come.

She brought a very curious instrument with a long tube attached. This she thrust down the Fourth Lady's throat, and instantly the rings came up. Everyone was much astonished except the foreigner, who packed her instrument and walked calmly away.

The other concubines were very angry with the Fourth Lady that she should have swallowed her good jade earrings. The fat one asked,

"And could you not have eaten a box of match heads, then, which may be bought for ten small cash?"

The Fourth Lady had nothing to say to this; they say that no one saw her eat or heard her speak while she was recovering. She lay on her bed with her curtains drawn. She has lost a great deal of face by being unsuccessful in her attempt. Indeed, it was for this my mother pitied her and sent her away to escape the taunts of the women.

Such matters, however, were mere small household gossip and had no place in the conversations I

held with my mother. It was only because I loved
the home so well that I felt I must know the details
of everything, and so I listened to the chatter of
Wang Da Ma. She has been with us so long that she
knows all our affairs. Indeed, she came with my
mother from her distant home in Shansi when my
father was married, and she it is who received into
her arms my mother's children at birth. When my
mother dies she will go to my brother's wife and
care for my mother's grandsons.

Only one matter heard thus was of more than
passing importance. My brother has determined to
go abroad, to America, for further study! My mother
said nothing of it to me, but Wang Da Ma told me
in whispers, when she brought the hot water the first
morning after my return, that my father had
laughed at his son's new ideas but in the end had
given his consent to his going because it has become
fashionable to send one's sons abroad for study, and
his friends are doing it. My mother was greatly distressed when she heard of it—more distressed than
she has been over anything in her life, Wang Da Ma
said, except when my father took his first concubine.
When she saw that my brother was really going she

refused food for three days and spoke to no one. At last seeing that he would go at any cost across the Peaceful Sea, she begged him to be married first to his betrothed, that she might bear a son. My mother said,

"Since you will not perceive that your flesh and blood are not yours alone, since you are willful and careless and run into the dangers of that barbarous country without consideration for your duty, at least transmit to another the sacred line of your ancestors, so that if you die—O my son!—at least I may behold my grandson!"

But my brother replied obstinately,

"I have no desire for marriage. I wish only to study more science and learn all concerning it. Nothing will happen to me, my mother. When I return—but not now—not now!"

Then my mother sent messages to our father, urging that he compel his son to marry. But my father was careless in the matter, being absorbed in the arrangements for the new concubine, and my brother had his own way.

I sympathized with my mother. This generation is the last of my father's line, since my grandfather had no other sons than my father. My mother's other sons died young, also, and it is therefore imperative that my brother as quickly as possible have a son, in order that my mother's duty may be performed to the ancestors. For this he has been betrothed since childhood to the daughter of Li. Although I have not seen her, it is true I have heard that she is not beautiful. But what is that in comparison to our mother's desires?

For several days I was troubled for my mother because of my brother's disobedience. But she never spoke of it to me. She buried this sadness, like all others, in the unseen places of her spirit. It has always been her way, when she perceived suffering to be inevitable, to close her lips upon it forever. Therefore I, surrounded by the familiar faces and walls, and accustomed to my mother's silences, gradually thought no more of my brother.

Of course the first thought I saw in all eyes was the one I feared and expected—what were my prospects of a son? Everyone asked the question, but I parried them all, merely accepting, with a grave inclination of my head, the good wishes given. No one should know that my husband did not care for me— no one. And yet I could not deceive my mother!

One night, after I had been at home for seven days, I sat idly in the doorway that opened into the large courtyard. It was twilight, and the slaves and the servants were bustling about the evening meals, and the odors of baked fish and brown duck were fragrant upon the air. It was just at the late edge of twilight, and in the courtyard the chrysanthemum plants were heavy with promise. The love of home and of old surroundings was warm within me. I laid my hand, I remember, upon the very carving of the door panel, loving it, feeling safe there where my childhood had passed so gently that, before I was aware, it was gone. It was all well beloved; the still dusk falling over the curved roofs, the candles beginning to gleam in the rooms, the spicy smell of food, and the voices of the children and the soft sound of their cloth shoes upon the tiles. Ah, I am the daughter of an old Chinese home, with old customs, old furniture, old well-tried relationships, safe, sure! I know how to live there!

Then I thought of my husband, sitting alone now

at the table in the foreign house, wearing his western clothes and looking an alien in every way. How
could I fit into his life? He had no need of me. My
throat was stiff with tears I could not shed. I was so
lonely, so much more lonely than I had ever been
as a girl. Then, as I have told you, My Sister, I looked
forward to the future. Now, the future had come to
pass. There was only bitterness in it. The tears would
force themselves out. I turned my head away toward
the twilight lest the candle light fall upon my cheeks
to betray me. Then the gong rang, and I was called
in to the meal. I wiped my eyes secretly and slipped
into my place.

My mother withdrew early to her room, and the
concubines went to their quarters. As I sat alone,
drinking my tea, suddenly Wang Da Ma appeared.

"Your honorable mother commands your presence," she said.

I wondered and said,

"But my mother has already told me she would
retire. She said nothing to me of any further speech."

"Nevertheless, she commands you. I have just come

from her room," rejoined Wang Da Ma; and she passed on without further explanation.

When her footsteps had receded into the court-yard I put aside the satin curtain and entered into my mother's room. To my surprise she was lying on the bed with a single tall candle lit on the table beside her. I had never seen her there in my life before. She looked exceedingly frail and tired. Her eyes were closed and her lips pale and drawn down. I went softly to the bedside and stood there. Her face was absolutely colorless, a grave, delicate face and very sad.

"My mother," I said gently.

"My child," she answered.

I hesitated, not knowing whether she wished me to sit or to remain standing. She put out her hand then, and motioned me to seat myself on the bed beside her. I obeyed and waited in silence until she wished to speak. I said within myself, "She is grieving for my brother in far countries."

But it was not of my brother she was thinking; instead she turned her face to me slightly and said,

"I perceive that all is not well with you, my daughter. Ever since you returned I have observed that your usual manner of quiet content is gone. You are restless in spirit, and tears come too easily to your eyes. It is as though some secret grief clung to your thoughts, although your lips do not speak of it. What is wrong? If it is that you are not yet with child, have patience. It was two years before I gave your father a son."

I did not know how to tell her. There was a bit of silk thread loosened from the embroidered curtain of the canopy, and this I twisted back and forth between my thumb and finger as, within, I twisted my thoughts.

"Speak!" she said somewhat sternly to me at last.

I looked at her, and oh, foolish, foolish tears! I could not utter a word for them. They welled up and welled up until I thought I had no breath with which to live. Then they burst forth in one hard sob and I buried my face in the quilt that covered my mother's body.

"Oh, I don't know what he means!" I cried. "He tells me to be equal with him, and I do not know how! He hates my feet and says they are ugly and draws such pictures! Although how he knows I cannot say, for I have never, never let him see them."

My mother sat up.

"Equal with him?" she said mystified, her eyes growing large in her pale face. "What does he mean? How can you be equal with your husband?"

"A woman is, in the West," I sobbed.

"Yes, but we are people of understanding here. And your feet? Why does he draw pictures of them? What do you mean?"

"To show me they are ugly," I whispered.

"Your feet? But surely you have been careless, then. I gave you twenty pairs of shoes. You have not chosen wisely."

"He does not draw the outside—it's the bones he draws, all crooked."

"Bones! Who has seen the bones in a woman's foot? Can a man's eyes pierce the flesh?"

"His can because he is a western doctor, he says."

"Ai-ya, my poor child!" My mother lay back again, sighing, and shook her head. "If he knows western magic—"

And then I found myself telling it all—all, until I whispered even these bitter words,

"He does not even care whether we have a son. He does not love me. O my mother, I am still a maid!"

There was a long silence. I hid my face again in the quilt.

I think I felt my mother's hand fall lightly on my head and remain for an instant—I cannot be sure; she was never one for outward signs. But at last she sat erect and began to speak.

"I cannot think that I have made a mistake in the manner in which you have been reared. I cannot think that you could fail to please a true Chinese gentleman. Can it be that you are married to a barbarian? Yet he is of the family of K'ung! Who could suspect it? It is the years abroad. I prayed to see your brother dead before he went to the outer countries!" She closed her eyes and lay back. Her thin face grew sharper.

When she spoke again, her voice was high and weak as though she were exhausted.

"Nevertheless, my child, there is only one path in

this world for a woman—only one path to follow at all costs. She must please her husband. It is more than I can bear that all my care for you must be undone. But you no longer belong to my family. You are your husband's. There is no choice left you save to be what he desires.—Yet, stay! Put forth once more every effort to beguile him. Clothe yourself in the jade green and black. Use the perfume of water-lilies. Smile—not boldly, but with the shyness that promises all. You may even touch his hand—cling to it for an instant. If he laughs, be gay. If he is still unmoved, then there is nothing left but to bend yourself to his will."

"Unbind my feet?" I whispered.

My mother was silent a space.

"Unbind your feet," she said wearily. "The times are changed. You are dismissed." And she turned her face to the wall.

✳✳✳✳✳✳✳✳✳✳✳✳✳✳✳✳✳✳

VI

How shall I tell of my heavy heart, My Sister?

The day of my departure dawned gray and still. It was near the end of the tenth moon, when brown leaves are beginning to drift silently to earth, and the bamboos shiver in the chill of dawn and sunset. I walked about the courtyards, lingering in the places I had long loved best and impressing their beauty freshly and more sharply upon my memory. I stood beside the pool listening to the faint wind crackling the dead pods and leaves of the lotus plants. I sat an hour beneath the gnarled juniper tree which for three hundred years has stood in the rock garden in the third court. I plucked a branch of the heavenly bamboo trees in the court of the great gate, delighting in the vivid scarlet berries hanging against the dark green leaves. And then, that I might have something to keep of all the beauty of the courts, I chose eight pots of chrysanthemums to take back with me.

They were at the moment of perfection, and I thought their red and gold and pale purple might mitigate a little the bareness of the house. Thus I returned to my husband.

He was not at home when I entered the little hall. The servant told me he had been called at sunrise by an urgent message, she did not know whither. I placed the chrysanthemums carefully about the little parlor, meditating how to dispose them to good advantage as a surprise for him. But when I had done my best I was disappointed. Richly as they had glowed in the old courtyard, against the black carvings of the passageways, here against whitewashed walls and yellow paint they faded to a mere artificial prettiness.

Ah, and so it was with me as well! I put on the jade satin trousers and coat and the black velvet sleeveless jacket. I dressed my hair with the jade and onyx ornaments, and I hung jade in my ears. I wore black shoes, made of velvet and cunningly wrought with tiny beads of gold. I had learned from La-may, the Fourth Lady in my mother's house, the guile of colorless cheeks and a lower lip touched with ver-

[73]

milion, and the witchery of scented, rosy palms. I
spared no pains for that first evening with my husband. I saw that I was beautiful.

When I was dressed, I sat waiting to hear his step
on the threshold. If I could have pushed aside a
scarlet satin curtain and appeared before him in the
subtle light of an old Chinese room, I might have
succeeded. But I had to come unsteadily down the
creaking stairway and then join him in that parlor.
There was nothing there to help me. I was like the
chrysanthemums—merely pretty.

As for my husband, he came in late and looked
very tired. By that time my own freshness had gone,
and although he greeted me kindly enough, his eyes
did not cling to me. He only asked that the servant
should hasten with the evening meal, because he had
been working all day with a sick person and had had
no food since morning.

We ate in silence. I could scarcely swallow for the
stupid tears, and he finished his rice hastily and then
sat frowning over his tea, with an occasional sigh.
At last he rose wearily and said,

"Let us go into the parlor."

We seated ourselves and he asked perfunctorily about my parents. He paid so little heed to my answers that I faltered in my endeavor to interest him and finally fell silent. At first he scarcely noticed that I had ceased to speak. Then he roused himself and said more kindly,

"I beg that you will not mind me. I am truly glad that you have returned. But this whole day I have been fighting against superstition and sheer stupidity, and I have lost. I can think of nothing else but that I have lost. I keep asking myself—did I do all that could be done? Was there an argument that I did not bring forward to save that life? But I think —I am sure—that I did everything—and still I lost!

"Do you remember the Yu family next to the Drum Tower? Their Second Lady tried to commit suicide to-day by hanging herself! It seems she could no longer endure the viperish tongue of her mother-in-law. They called me in and, mind you, I could have saved her! She had only just let go the rope when they found her—only just! I prepared the remedies at once. Then in came the aged uncle who is a wine merchant. Old Mr. Yu, you remember, is dead, and the wine merchant is the head of the family now. He came in blustering and angry and at once demanded that the old methods should be used. He sent for the priests to beat the gongs to call the woman's soul back, and her relatives gathered about and placed the poor unconscious girl—she is not twenty yet—into a kneeling position on the floor; then they deliberately filled her nose and mouth with cotton and cloth and bound clothing around her face!"

"But—but—" I said, "it is the custom—it is what is always done. You see, so much of the spirit is already escaped that they must keep the rest in by closing the orifices."

He had begun to walk around the room in his agitation. Now he stopped before me, his lips pressed together. I could hear his quick breathing. He actually glared at me.

"What!" he shouted. "You, too?"

I shrank back.

"Did she die?" I whispered.

"Die? Would you die if I did this long enough?" and he seized my hands in one of his and placed his handkerchief roughly over my mouth and nose.

I twisted free and tore it away. He gave a laugh as hard as a dog's bark and sat down with his head in his hands, and we remained in silence as heavy as pain. He never saw the chrysanthemums I had arranged with such care about the room.

I sat watching him, bewildered and a little frightened. Could it be that he was right, after all?

That night I laid the jade ornaments sorrowfully in their silver case and put the satin garments away. I had been taught all wrong, I began to realize. My husband was not one of those men to whom a woman is as distinctly an appeal to the sense as a perfumed flower or a pipe of opium. The refinement of beauty in body was not enough. I must study to please him in other ways. I remembered my mother, with her face turned to the wall, and her weary voice, saying,

"The times have changed."

※

Still I could not bring myself easily to the unbinding of my feet. It was really Mrs. Liu who helped me. She was the wife of a teacher in a new foreign school. I had heard my husband speak of Mr. Liu as his friend. She sent word the day after my return that if it pleased me she would call the following day.

I made great preparations for she was my first caller. I directed the servant to buy six kinds of cakes as well as watermelon seeds and sesame wafers and the best Before-the-Rains tea. I wore my apricot pink satin and placed pearls in my ears. Secretly I was very much ashamed of the house. I feared she would think it ugly and wonder at my taste. I hoped that my husband would not be at home so that I might at least place the chairs and table more formally and thus show distinctly which was the place of honor.

But for once he did not go out. He sat reading and glanced up with a smile as I entered the room a little nervously. I had planned to be seated when the guest came and as the servant ushered her in, to rise and bow her to the best seat. But with my husband there I had no chance to arrange the room, and when the bell rang, my husband himself went to the door. I was most chagrined and wrung my hands and wondered what to do. I heard a cheerful voice then, and I could not help peeping into the hall. I beheld a strange thing. My husband had taken the guest's hand and was shaking it up and down in the most peculiar manner. I was amazed.

Then suddenly my astonishment and all thought of the guest dropped from me, for I looked at his face. O my husband, never had thy face worn that look for me, thy wife! It was as if at last he had found a friend.

O My Sister, had you been here you might have taught me what to do! But I was alone. I had no friends. I could only ponder and grieve within myself and wonder what I lacked to please him.

And the while she was there I examined my guest closely to see if she were beautiful. But she was not beautiful or even pretty. Her face was large and red and good-humored, and her eyes, though kindly and crinkling with smiles, were round and bright like glass beads. She wore a coat of plain gray cloth over a black unflowered silk skirt, and her feet were shod like men's. Her voice was pleasant, however, and her speech came swiftly and readily, and her laughter was warm and quick. She talked a great deal with my husband, and I sat listening with drooping head. They spoke of things of which I had never heard. Foreign words flew back and forth between them. I understood nothing except the pleasure on my husband's face.

❋

That night I sat silent with my husband after the evening meal. My mind returned again and again to the look on his face during the visit. Never before had I seen on it an expression like that—so eager, so alight! He was full of words for her—he poured them out as he stood before her. He remained in the room throughout her visit as though she were a man.

I rose and went to his side.

"Yes?" he asked, looking up from his book.

"Tell me about the lady who called to-day," I asked.

He leaned back in his chair and looked at me reflectively.

"What about her? She is a graduate of a big western college for women called Vassar. She is clever and interesting, as one likes a woman to be. Besides, she is rearing three magnificent boys—intelligent, clean, well cared for. It does my heart good to see them."

Oh, I hate her—I hate her! Oh, what can I do? Is there only one way to his heart?—She was not pretty at all—

"Do you think her pretty?" I whispered.

"Well, yes, I do," he answered stoutly. "She is healthy and sensible and walks on sound, steady feet."

He stared into space. I thought desperately for a few minutes. There was only one way for women. How could I—and yet my mother's words were, "You must please your husband."

My husband sat staring thoughtfully across the room. I did not know what was in his mind. But I knew this; although I wore peach-colored satin and had pearls in my ears, although my hair was smooth and black and shining in cunningly arranged coils, although I stood at his shoulder so close that a slight motion of his body would have brought his hand to mine, yet he was not thinking of me.

Then I hung my head lower and gave myself into his hands. I renounced my past. I said,

"If you will tell me how, I will unbind my feet."

※※※※※※※※※※※※※※※※※※

VII

WHEN I look back now, I realize that my husband's
interest began in me that evening. It seemed as
though before this we had nothing to talk about.
Our thoughts never met. I could only watch him
wondering and not understanding, and he never
looked at me at all. When we spoke it was with the
courtesy of strangers to each other, I with shyness
towards him, he with careful politeness that over-
looked me. But now that I had need of him he saw
me at last, and when he spoke he questioned me and
cared to hear my answer. As for me, the love that
had been trembling in my heart for him steadied
into adoration then. I had never dreamed that a man
could stoop so tenderly to a woman.

When I asked him how I could unbind my feet, I
thought, of course, that he would merely give me
directions from his medical knowledge. And so I sat

astounded when he himself fetched a basin of hot water and a roll of white bandage. I was ashamed. I could not endure having him see my feet. No one had seen them since I was old enough to care for them myself. Now, when he set the basin on the floor and knelt to take my feet, my whole body burned.

"No," I said faintly. "I will do it myself."

"You must not mind," he answered. "I am a doctor, you remember."

Still I refused. Then he looked me steadfastly in the face.

"Kwei-lan," he said gravely, "I know it costs you something to do this for me. Let me help you all I can. I am your husband."

Without a word then, I yielded. He took my foot, and gently he withdrew the shoe and the stocking and unwound the inner cloth. His expression was sad and stern.

"How you have suffered!" he said in a low, tender voice; "how wretched a childhood—and all for nothing!"

[83]

The tears came into my eyes at his words. He was making useless all the sacrifice, and even demanding a new sacrifice!

✻

For when my feet had been soaked and bound again more loosely, intolerable suffering set in. Indeed, the unbinding process was almost as painful as the binding had been. My feet, accustomed to constriction, gradually stretched a little, and the blood began to circulate.

There were times in the day when I tore at the bandages to unfasten them and bind them more tightly to ease me; and then the thought of my husband and that he would know at night made me replace them with trembling hands. The only slight respite I could get was to sit on my feet and rock back and forth.

No longer did I care how I appeared before my husband, or look in the mirror to see if I were at least fresh and neat. At night my eyes were swollen with weeping, and my voice rough with sobs I could not control. Strange that when my beauty could not move him, my distress did! He would comfort me as though I were a child. I clung to him often without realizing in my pain who or what he was.

"We will endure this together, Kwei-lan," he said. "It is hard to see you suffer so. Try to think that it is not only for us but for others, too—a protest against an old and wicked thing."

"No!" I sobbed, "I do it only for you—to be a modern woman for you!"

He laughed and his face lighted a little, as it had when he talked to that other woman. This was my reward for pain. Nothing seemed quite so hard afterwards.

❈

And indeed, as the flesh grew more healthy, I began to know a new freedom. I was young, and my feet were yet sound. Often in older women bound feet will mortify and sometimes even drop away. But mine were only numbed. Now I began to walk more freely, and the stairs were not so difficult. I felt stronger all over my body. One evening I ran without thinking into the room where my husband was writing. He looked up in surprise, and his face broke into a smile.

"Running?" he exclaimed. "Ah, well, we are over the worst then, and the bitterness is eaten."

I looked at my feet in surprise.

"But they are not yet as large as Mrs. Liu's," I said.

"No, they never can be," he replied. "Hers are natural feet. Yours are as large as we can get them, now."

I felt a little sorrowful that my feet could never be as large as hers. But I thought of a way. Since all my little embroidered shoes were useless now, I determined to get some new leather ones like Mrs. Liu's. The next day, therefore, I went with a servant to a shop and bought a pair of shoes the length I wished. They were two inches longer than my feet, but I stuffed the toes hard with cotton. When I put on the shoes no one could tell I had had bound feet.

I was anxious to have Mrs. Liu see them, and I asked my husband when I might return her call.

"I will go with you to-morrow," he said.

I was surprised that he would be willing to go on the street with me. It is certainly not good custom, and it embarrassed me not a little, but I have grown more used now to his doing strange things.

We went the next day therefore, and my husband treated me most kindly in her presence. True, he confused me greatly once or twice, as for instance, when he made me precede him into the room where Mrs. Liu was. I did not know his meaning at the time. After we came home, he explained that it was the western manner.

"Why?" I asked. "Is it because, as I have heard, that men are inferior to women over there?"

"No," he answered, "that is not true."

Then he explained it to me. It is grounded, he said, in an old system of courtesy which began in ancient times. This was very astonishing to me. I did not know that there were ancient people except ours, that is, civilized people. But it seems that foreigners also have a history and a culture. They are therefore not wholly barbarian. My husband promised to read me some books about them.

I felt happy that night when I went to bed. It was interesting to be a little more modern. For not only had I worn my leather shoes that day, but I had not painted my face or put ornaments in my hair. I looked very much like Mrs. Liu. I am sure my husband noticed it.

❅

It seemed that, once I was willing to change, a complete new life poured in upon me. My husband began to talk to me in the evening, and I found his conversation very exciting. He knows everything. *Yoh!* The queer things he has told me about the outer countries and their inhabitants! He laughed when I exclaimed,

"Oh, funny—oh, strange!"

"No more strange than we are to them," he said, for some reason greatly amused.

"What!" I cried in fresh astonishment. "Do they think we are funny?"

"Of course," he replied, still laughing. "You should hear them talk! They think our clothes are funny and our faces and our food and all that we do. It does not occur to them that people can look as we do and behave as we do, and be wholly as human as they are."

I was astounded to hear this. How could they consider their curious looks and clothes and behavior as human as ours? I answered with dignity,

"But we have always done these things and had these customs and looked as we do, with black hair and eyes—"

"Exactly! So have they!"

"But I thought they came over here to our country to learn civilization. My mother said so."

"She was mistaken. In fact, I believe they come over here thinking to teach us civilization. They have a great deal to learn from us, it is true, but they don't know it any more than you realize what we have to learn from them."

Certainly it was all very novel and interesting, what he had to say. I never grew weary of hearing about the foreigners, and especially did I like to hear of all their marvelous inventions: of turning a handle and getting hot or cold water out of it, and of a stove with no fuel that one could see, and yet having heat—self-coming water and self-coming heat, these are called. And how amazed was I at his stories of machines on the sea and of others flying in the air and floating under the water and many like marvels!

"You are sure it is not magic?" I asked fearfully. "The old books tell of miracles of fire and earth and

water but they are always the magic tricks of creatures partly faërie."

"No, of course it is not magic," he replied. "It is
all quite simple when you understand how it is done.
It is science."

That science again! It made me think of my
brother. For the sake of that science he is still in
these foreign countries, eating their food and drinking their water to which his body is not accustomed
by birth. I became very curious to see this science
and know what it looks like. But when I said this
my husband laughed a great deal.

"What a child you are!" he cried, teasing me. "It
is not a thing you can handle or touch or take in
your hands to examine like a toy."

Then seeing that I perceived nothing of what he
meant, he went to the bookcase and brought forth
some books with pictures upon the pages, and he
began to explain to me many things.

Thereafter, every evening he taught me concerning this science. No wonder my brother became en-
tranced of it so that he would not heed even his
mother's desires, but would go across the Peaceful

Sea in search of it. I was enchanted of it myself and began to feel myself growing marvelously wise. So much so that at last I felt I must tell someone, and having no one else, I told our old cook-woman.

"Do you know," I asked her, "that the world is round and that our great country is, after all, not in the middle, but only a patch of earth and water on the skin, together with the other countries?"

She was washing the rice in the small pond in the kitchen yard, but she stopped shaking the basket and looked at me suspiciously.

"Who says this?" she demanded, in no hurry to be convinced.

"Our master," I said firmly. "Now will you believe me?"

"Oh," she replied doubtfully, "he knows a great deal. Still, you can tell the world is not round just by looking at it. See, if you climb to the top of the pagoda on the Hill of the North Star, you can see for a thousand miles of mountain and field and lake and river, and it is all as flat as sheets of dried bean curd, except for the mountains, and no one could call them round! As for our country, it must be in the middle. Else why did the wise ancients, who knew everything, call it the Middle Kingdom?"

But I was eager to proceed.

"More than that," I continued, "the earth is so large that it takes the whole length of a moon to reach the other side, and when it is dark here the sun is over there giving light."

"Now I know you are wrong, my mistress," she cried triumphantly. "If it takes a moon of days to get to those other countries, how can the sun do it in an hour when he spends a whole day in traveling the short space here between Purple Mountain and the Western Hills?"

And she fell to shaking the basket of rice in the water again.

But really I could not blame her for her ignorance; for of all the curious things my husband told me the most curious is this, that the western peoples have the same three great lights of heaven that we have—the sun, the moon, and the stars. I had always thought that P'an-ku, the creator god, had made them for the Chinese. But my husband is wise. He knows all things, and he speaks only what is true.

※※※※※※※※※※※※※※※※※※

VIII

How may I put into words the beginning of my husband's favor towards me, My Sister? How did I know it myself when his heart stirred?

Ah, how does the cold earth know when the sun at spring-tide draws out her heart into blossoming? How does the sea feel the moon compelling her to him?

I do not know how the days passed. Only I knew that I ceased to be lonely. Where he was became my home, and I thought no more of my mother's house.

During the lingering hours of the day in his absence I pondered over all my husband's words. I remembered his eyes, his face, the curve of his lips, the casual touch of his hand against mine as he turned the page of the book on the table before us. When night came and he was there before me, I glanced at him secretly, and I fed my heart upon his looks as he taught me.

Day and night I thought of him until, like the river in spring-time flowing richly into the canals empty with the drought of winter, like the river flowing into the land and filling everything with life and fruition, so did the thought of my lord become to me, filling my every loneliness and need.

Who can understand this power in a man and a maid? It begins with a chance meeting of the eyes, a shy and lingering glance, and then suddenly it flames into a fixed and burning gaze. There is a touch of fingers at first quickly withdrawn, and then heart rushes to heart.

But how may I tell even you, My Sister? It was the time of my great joy. These words I speak now are scarlet words. On the last day of the eleventh moon I knew that when the rice harvest came, in the fullness of the year, my child would be born.

When I told my husband that I had fulfilled my duty towards him in conception, he was very happy. He gave formal notice to his parents first and then to his brothers, and we received their congratulations. My own parents of course were not immediately concerned in the matter, but I determined to tell my mother when I visited her at New Year.

Now began a most difficult time for me. Hitherto I had been person of little importance in my husband's family. I had been merely the wife of one of the younger sons. I had had almost no share in the family life since we moved away from the great home. Twice I had gone at stated seasons to pay my respects and serve tea to my husband's mother, but she had treated me negligently, although not unkindly. Now suddenly I became as a priestess of destiny. Within me I bore the hope of the family, an heir. My husband was one of six sons, none of whom had male offspring. Should my child be a son, therefore, he would rank next to my husband's eldest brother in the family and the clan, and he would be the heir of the family estates. Oh, it is the sorrow of a mother that her son is hers but the first few brief days! Too soon he must take his place in the great family life. My son can be mine such a short, short while! O Kwan-yin, protect my little child!

[95]

The ecstasy of the hour when my husband and I first spoke of the child was soon gone in the anxiety that pressed upon us. I have said it was a difficult time for me. It was because of the much advice I received from everyone. Most important were the words I received from my revered mother-in-law.

When she heard of my joy, she sent for me to come to her. Hitherto when I had visited her I had been received formally in the guest-hall, for she had been a little haughty towards us since we moved away. This time, however, she had evidently commanded the servant to lead me to the family room behind the third court.

There I found my mother-in-law seated by the table, drinking tea and waiting for me. She is a majestic old lady, very fat, with tiny feet long since inadequate for her great weight. Now if she walks so much as a single step, she leans heavily on two stout slave-girls who stand ever ready behind her chair. Her hands are small and covered with gold rings and so plump that the fingers stick out stiffly from the mound of dimpled flesh. She holds always a long pipe of polished silver, which her slaves keep filled for her and light from a twist of paper, smoldering and ready to be blown into a flame in an instant for her use.

I went to her immediately and bowed before her. She smiled so that her narrow lips disappeared into the fullness of her heavy cheeks, and then she took my hand and patted it.

"Good daughter—good daughter," she said in her husky voice. Long since her neck has disappeared in rolls of flesh, and her voice is always asthmatic.

I knew I had pleased her. I poured out tea into a bowl and presented it to her with both hands, and she received it. Then I sat down upon a small side seat. But she would not allow such humbleness in me now, although before she had not cared where I sat. Smiling and coughing, she beckoned me to sit in the seat next her on the opposite side of the table, and at her command I did so.

She sent then for her other daughters-in-law, and they all came in to congratulate me. Three of them had never conceived, although married several years, and to these I was an envy and a reproach. Indeed, the eldest one, a tall, yellow-faced woman always ailing and ill, began to wail loudly now and to rock back and forth and bemoan her fate.

"Ai-ya—ai-ya—a bitter life—an evil destiny!"

My mother-in-law sighed and shook her head gravely and allowed her eldest daughter-in-law to comfort herself with weeping for the space of two pipes of tobacco. Then she bade her be still, since she wished to speak with me. Later I learned that my husband's eldest brother had just taken a second wife, since his first had never borne him any children. It was this that made acute the poor creature's grief that day, because she loved her husband, and because she knew at last that her prayers and sacrifices to the gods were unnoticed by them.

My mother-in-law gave me much sound advice. Among other things she told me not to prepare any clothes before the child's birth. This was the custom in her girlhood home in Anhwei, where people believed that it served to keep the cruel gods unaware of the approaching birth lest, seeing a man born into the world, they would seek to destroy him. But when I heard of the custom I inquired,

"What then shall he wear, a little naked, new-born child?"

"Wrap him," she said ponderously, "in his father's oldest clothes. It will bring luck to do that. I did it with my six sons and they lived."

My sisters-in-law also bade me do many, many things, and each one gave me the custom of her home in these matters. Particularly did they advise me to eat a certain kind of fish after the child was born and to drink bowls of brown sugar and water. Thus did each one ease her own envy of me with advice.

❋

When I returned to my husband in the evening happy in all this friendly interest of his family, I told him of these things they had bidden me do for the child. To my horrified surprise he suddenly became violently angry. He pushed his hair about with his hands, and he strode about the room.

"Nonsense—nonsense—nonsense!" he cried. "All lies—all superstition—never, never!" He stopped and took me by the shoulders and looked earnestly into my upturned face. "Promise me," he said firmly,

[99]

"that you will be guided wholly by me. Mind you, you must obey! Kwei-lan, promise me, or I swear there will never be another child!"

What could I do in my fright but promise?

When I had given my word dubiously he became more calm. He said,

"To-morrow I will take you to a western home, to see the family of my old teacher who is an American. I want you to see how westerners care for their children, not that you may copy them slavishly, but that you may enlarge your ideas."

I tried to obey my husband. One thing only did I do in secret. Next morning at dawn I slipped out of the house with none but a servant to accompany me. I bought sticks of incense at the shop, where it was so early that only a yawning little apprentice boy was stirring in the dim misty morning. Then I went to the temple, and lighting the incense I placed it before the little dark Kwan-yin who gives sons and easy child-birth. I knocked my head upon the marble slab before her. It was still wet with the dews of night. I murmured what was in my heart and rose and looked at her, beseeching. She did not respond, and the urn was full of cold ashes of incense that other mothers had placed there before me, with prayers and longing like mine. I thrust into the ashes more firmly the sticks of incense I had lit, and left them there burning before her. Then I returned to my home.

True to his word, the next day my husband took me to visit the home of his foreign friends. I was not a little curious, and I was even a little afraid. I smile at that now, I who call you My Sister!

But then I had never been in a foreign house. I had no opportunity. I never walked abroad upon the streets, and no one in my mother's home associated with foreigners. My father had seen them, of course, in his travels, and he considered them of no importance except to make him laugh with their coarse looks and abrupt, rude ways. Only my brother admired them strangely. He had often seen them in Peking, and in his school there were some foreigners who were his teachers. Once I had even heard it said before my marriage that he had been in the house of a foreigner, and I admired his daring then, very much.

But in my mother's home there was no such intercourse. Sometimes a servant going forth to make a purchase would come back and say in excitement that she had seen a foreigner on the street passing by, and then there would be wondering talk of their strange livid skin and pale eyes. I always listened in the same curiosity and fear that I had when Wang Da Ma told me of the ghosts and devils of ancient times. The servants, indeed, even whispered about the black magic of these foreigners and their power of stealing the soul out of a person with a little machine in a black box, into which they peered with one eye. When something snapped inside the box, one felt a curious weakness in the breast, and then always soon after illness or accident would come bringing death.

But my husband laughed greatly when I told him of all these things.

"How then did I come back alive after twelve years in their country?" he asked.

"Ah, but you are wise—you learned their magic,"
I replied.

"Come and see for yourself what they are like,"
he answered. "They are men and women like all
others."

And so on that same day we went, and we entered
into a garden with grass and trees and flowers. I
was surprised that it was so beautiful and that
westerners understood the value of nature. Of course
the arrangement of all was very crude—no courts
or gold-fish ponds, but trees planted in any way and
flowers growing irregularly as they pleased. I must
confess that when at last we stood before the door
of the house, I should have run away had not my
husband been there with me.

The door was opened suddenly from within, and a
tall male "foreign devil" stood there, smiling all
across his large face. I knew he was a man because
he wore clothes like my husband's, but to my
horror, his head, instead of being covered with
human hair, black and straight like that of other
people, had on it a fuzzy red wool! His eyes were

like pebbles washed by the sea, and his nose rose up a very mountain in the middle of his face. Oh, he was a frightful creature to behold—more hideous than the God of the North in the temple entrance!

My husband is brave. He did not seem at all disturbed by the sight of this man; he held out his hand, and the foreigner grasped it and moved it up and down. My husband was not surprised by this, and turning to me, he introduced me. The foreigner smiled his enormous smile and made as if to take my hand also. But I looked at his out-stretched one. It was large and bony, and upon it were long red hairs and black spots. My flesh shrank. I could not touch it. I placed my hands in my sleeves and bowed. He smiled still more widely then, and invited us to enter.

We went into a small hall like our own and then into a room. Beside the window sat a person whom I discerned at once to be a female foreigner. At least, she wore a long cotton gown instead of trousers and had a flat string about her middle. Her hair was not as ugly as her husband's, for it was smooth and straight, although of an unfortunate yellow color. She also had a very high nose, although it was not curved like her husband's, and large hands

with short square nails. I looked at her feet and saw
that they were like rice-flails for size. I thought to
myself,

"With parents like these, what must the little foreign devils be?"

I have to say, however, that these foreigners were
as polite as they knew how to be. They made mis-
takes and at every turn betrayed their lack of breed-
ing. They presented the bowls of tea with one hand
and habitually served me before my husband. The
man actually addressed me to my face! I felt it an
insult. He should have courteously ignored my presence, leaving his wife to entertain me.

One cannot blame them, I suppose. Yet they have
been here twelve years, my husband tells me. One
would think that something must be learned in that
time. Of course you, My Sister, have lived here always, and you are now one of us.

But the most interesting part of the visit came
when my husband asked the foreign woman to let
me see her children and their clothes. We were ex-
pecting a child of our own, he explained, so that he
wished me to see western ways. She rose at once and
asked me to go upstairs. I was afraid to go alone

with her. I looked at my husband in appeal, but he only nodded to me to proceed.

I forgot about fear, however, as soon as I was upstairs. She took me into a sun-flooded room that was warmed with a black oven. It was curious that although they evidently wanted to heat the room, they left a window ajar so that cold air came in constantly. But these details I did not notice at once. I saw first, with the utmost sense of fascination, three little foreigners playing upon the floor. I had never seen such queer little creatures!

They were healthy in appearance and fat, but they all had white hair. This confirmed what I had heard, that foreigners reverse our nature and are born with snow-white hair which darkens as they grow older. They had very white skin. I supposed it was washed in some sort of medicine water until the mother showed me a room where they were all washed entirely every day. This then explained their skin. The tints of nature were faded out with so much washing.

The mother showed me also their clothes. All their underclothes were white, and, indeed, the youngest child was dressed in white from head to foot. I asked the mother if the child were in mourning for some relative, since white is the color of grief, but she replied that it was not this, but only that the child might be kept clean. I thought a dark color would have been better, since white is so easily soiled. But I observed everything and said nothing.

Then I saw their beds. They were also covered in white and were most depressing. I could not understand why so much white was used. It is the sad hue of mourning and death. Surely a child should be clad and covered only with the colors of joy, scarlet and yellow and royal blue! We clothe our babies in scarlet from head to foot for joy that they are born to us. But nothing about these foreigners is according to nature.

One of the surprising things I discovered was that the foreign woman nursed her own child at the breast. I had not thought of nursing mine. It is not customary among women of any wealth or position, since slaves are abundant for this task.

After we had come home I told my husband everything. At last I said,

"She even nurses her own child. Are they, then, so very poor?"

"It is good to nurse the child," said my husband. "You shall nurse yours, too."

"What, I?" I answered in great surprise.

"Certainly," he replied gravely.

"But then I shall not have another child for two years," I objected.

"That is as it should be," rejoined my husband, "although the reason you give is nonsense."

Perhaps he is right in this also. At any rate I perceive that since several children of every family must inevitably die and some must be girls, that I shall not have my house as full of sons as I had hoped. Do you marvel, My Sister, that I never ceased to find my husband strange?

❋

The next day I went to see Mrs. Liu to tell her of my visit. Ah, if the goddess grants me a son like her children—straight and ruddy and shining-eyed! They were beautiful and golden-skinned, exquisite in their red and flowered clothes.

"You have kept to our old customs," I said, observing the children with a sigh of pleasure.

"Yes—no—look!" she replied, and she pulled the eldest child toward her. "See, my white is all inside—linings which can be taken out and washed. Learn the good that you can of the foreign people and reject the unsuitable."

I went from her house to the cloth shop. I bought red and pink flowered silk of the softest quality, and black velvet for a tiny sleeveless jacket, and satin for a cap. It was hard to choose, since I would have nothing but the best for my son. I commanded the owner of the shop to pull down more and yet more of the silk he had folded away in dark paper covers and placed in the shelves that reached to the ceiling. He was an old man hard of breathing, and he grumbled when I cried,

"Show me yet more—a piece of silk with peach flowers embroidered upon it!"

I heard him mutter something of the vanity of women and hearing him I said,

"It is not for myself but for my son."

Then he smiled crookedly and brought me the

loveliest piece of all, the piece he had withheld until now.

"Take it," he said. "I was keeping it for the magistrate's wife, but if it is for your son, take it. She is but a woman after all."

It was the piece I sought. Among the vivid piles of silks scattered over the counter it shone with a deep rosy luster. I bought it without questioning the price, although I know the cunning old man added to it, seeing my eagerness. I carried it in my arms to my home. I said,

"To-night I shall cut from this the little coat and trousers. I shall do it all alone. I am jealous of another's touch upon my child."

Oh, I was so happy I could have sewed the night through for my son! I have made him a pair of shoes with tiger faces. I have bought him a silver chain for his pleasure.

❉❉❉❉❉❉❉❉❉❉❉❉❉❉❉❉❉

IX

IT is you? I have great news! To-day my son leaped at my heart! It is as though he had spoken.

I have prepared his little clothes. The garments are complete even to the tiny gold Buddhas stitched about his satin cap. When all were finished and perfect I bought a sandalwood chest and placed the clothes in it that they might be filled with sweet perfume for my son's flesh. Now I have no more to do, although the rice is still jade-green in the fields, and I have three more moons to wait. I sit and dream of how he will look.

O little dusky Goddess! Speed the winged days, I pray thee, until my golden one is in my arms!

At least for one day he shall be my own. I will not think beyond that. For my husband's parents have sent us a letter telling us that the child must return to his ancestral home. He is the only grandson, and his life is too precious to be away from the sight of his grandparents, night and day. Already they hang on the thought of him fondly. My husband's father, who has never spoken a word to me, sent for me the other day and talked with me, and I could see that to his aged mind it was as though his grandson were already born.

Oh, I long to keep him to ourselves! I am reconciled to the little foreign house and the strange ways if we can keep our son here, just the three of us. But I know the proper traditions of our people. It is not to be supposed that I may have my first-born for my own. He belongs to all the family.

My husband is most unhappy about it. He frowns and mutters that the child will be ruined by foolish slave-girls and overmuch feeding and harmful luxury. He paces the floor, and once he even grieved that the child was to be born. I was frightened then lest the gods grow angry at his ingratitude, and I begged him to be silent.

"We must endure what is the right custom," I told him, my heart aching the while with longing to keep my child.

But now he has become quiet again and very grave. He speaks no more concerning his parents. I wonder what he has determined upon in his mind, that he does not speak! But as for me, I think no further now than that day when the little precious one shall be here for me to feast my eyes upon.

I know now what my husband has done. Do you think it wrong, My Sister? Oh, I do not know myself—I can only trust that it is right because he does it. He has told his parents that, even as he claimed his wife for himself alone, so now he requires that his son shall belong to his own parents only—to us!

His parents were angry, but we could bear their anger, answering nothing. But my husband said that at last his old father gave up his arguments and fell to weeping silently, and when I heard of that it seemed a piteous thing that a son should make his father weep. If it had been anything except this, except my son, my heart would have weakened in my breast. But my husband is braver than I, and he even bore the pity of his father's weeping.

Ah, when we first moved away from his father's house I reproached him for breaking the honored customs of the past. But now, selfish woman that I am, I do not care that the tradition is broken. I think only of my son. He will be mine—mine! I need not share him with twenty others—his grandparents, his aunts. I, his mother, may care for him; I may wash him and clothe him and keep him at my side day and night.

Now has my husband recompensed me for everything. I thank the gods that I am married to a modern man. He gives me my son for my own. All my life is not enough to repay my gratitude.

Daily I watch the rice grow yellow in the fields. The heads are full now and drooping. A little longer under this languorous sun and they will be bursting with ripeness and ready for the harvest. It is a good year in which my son is to be born—a full year, the farmers say.

How many more days of dreamy waiting?

I have ceased to think whether my husband loves

me. When I have given birth to his son, my husband will know my heart and I shall know his.

O My Sister, My Sister! He is here, my son is here! He lies in the curve of my arm at last, and his hair is as black as ebony!

Look at him—it is not possible that such beauty has been created before. His arms are fat and dimpled, and his legs like young oak-trees for strength. I have examined his whole body for love. It is as sound and fair as the child of a god. Ah, the rogue! He kicks and cries to be at the breast, and he has eaten but an hour ago! His voice is lusty, and he demands everything.

Oh, but my hour was hard, My Sister! My husband watched me with fond and anxious eyes. I paced before the window in my joy and agony. They were cutting the ripe grain and laying it in rich sheaves upon the ground. The fullness of the year— the fullness of life!

I gasped at the snarling pain and then exulted to

know that I was at the height of my womanhood.
Thus I gave birth to my first-born son! Ai-ya, but
he was a sturdy one! How he forced the gates of life
into the world, and with what a mighty cry did he
come forth! I feared to die with the pain of his impatience, and then I gloried in his strength. My
golden man-child!

Now has my life flowered. Shall I tell you all, that
you may know how complete is my joy? Why
should I not say it to you, My Sister, who have
seen thus far my naked heart? It was like this, then.

I lay weak and yet in triumph upon my bed. My
son was at my side. My husband entered the room.
He approached the bedside and reached out his
arms. My heart leaped. He wished for the old custom
of presentation.

I took my son, and I placed him in his father's
arms. I presented him with these words,

"My dear lord, behold thy firstborn son. Take
him. Thy wife gives him to thee."

He gazed into my eyes. I was faint with the ardent
light of his regard. He bent nearer to me. He spoke,

"I give him back to thee. He is ours." His voice

was low and his words fell through the air like drops of silver. "I share him with thee. I am thy husband who loves thee!"

You weep, My Sister? Ah, yes, I know—I, too! How else how could we bear such joy? See my son! He laughs!

PART TWO

❋❋❋❋❋❋❋❋❋❋❋❋❋❋❋❋❋❋

X

'O MY SISTER, I thought that now, since my son is /0
here, forever would I have only joyful words to
speak to you. I was triumphant and sure that nothing could come near me to make me sorrowful
again. How is it that so long as there are bonds of
blood there may be pain come from them?

To-day my heart can hardly bear its own throbbing. No—no—it is not my son! He has had nine
months of life now, and he is a very Buddha for
fatness. You have not seen him since he desired to
stand upon his legs. Ah, it is enough to make a monk
laugh! Since he perceived he could walk he is
angered if anyone wishes him to sit. Indeed, in my
arms there is not strength enough to bend him. His
thoughts are full of lovely mischief, and his eyes
dance with light. His father says he is spoiled, but I
ask you, how can I scold such a one, who melts me
with his willfulness and beauty, so that I am filled

with tears and laughter? Ah, no—it is never my son!

No, it is that brother of mine. I speak of him who is the only son of my mother, he who has been these three years in America. It is he who pours out the blood from my mother's heart and from my heart like this.

You remember I told you of him—how in my childhood I loved him? But I have not seen him now for these many years, and I have heard of him even only a very little because my mother has never forgotten that against her will he left her home; and even when she commanded him to marry his betrothed he would not. His name does not rise easily to her lips.

And now he is disturbing the quiet of her life again. He is not satisfied that he has already disobeyed his mother gravely in the past. Now he must —but see, here is the letter! It came a day ago by the hand of Wang Da Ma, our old nurse, who fed us both at her breast when we were born and who has known every affair of my mother's family.

When she entered she bowed her head to the floor before my son. Presenting this letter to me she wept

and cried out with three deep groans, saying, "Aie
—Aie—Aie—"

Then I, knowing that only catastrophe could cause
this, felt my life stop in my breast for a second's
space.

"My mother—my mother!" I cried.

I remembered how feebly she had leaned upon
her staff when I last saw her. I reproached myself
inwardly that I had gone to her but twice since the
child's birth. I had been too absorbed in my own
happiness.

"It is not your mother, Daughter of the most
Honorable Lady," she replied, sighing heavily. "The
gods have prolonged her life to see this sorrow."

"Is my father—" I asked, quick terror changing to
anxiety.

"That honorable one also drinks not yet of the
Yellow Springs," she replied, bowing.

"Then?" I asked, seeing the letter she had placed
on my knee.

She pointed to it.

"Let the young mother of a princely son read the
letter," she suggested. "It is written within."

Then I bade the servant pour tea for her in the

outer room, and giving my son to his attendant I looked at the letter. Its superscription was my name, and the name of the sender, my mother. I was filled with wonder. She had never written a letter to me before.

When I had marveled for a time, I opened the narrow envelope and drew out the thin sheet from within. Upon it I saw the delicate, studied lines of my mother's writing-brush. I passed hastily over the formal opening sentences, and then my eyes fell upon these words, and they were the kernel of the letter,

"Your brother, who has been in foreign countries these many months, now writes me that he wishes to take in marriage a foreign female."

Then the formal closing sentences. That was all. But, O My Sister, I could feel my mother's heart bleeding through the scanty words! I cried aloud,

"O cruel and insane brother—O wicked and cruel son!" until the maidservants hastened in to comfort me and to beg me remember that anger would poison my milk for the child.

Then seeing that I was seized with so great a flood

of tears that I could not stem it, they sat down upon the floor and wept loudly with me, in order to drain my rage from me. When I had wept myself to calmness and had wearied of their noise, I bade them be silent and I sent for Wang Da Ma. I said to her,

"Wait yet another hour until my son's father comes home that I may open the letter before him and know what he would bid me do. I will ask permission to go to my mother. Meanwhile, eat rice and meat for your refreshment."

She willingly agreed, and I gave orders that an extra bit of pork be placed before her, taking my comfort in consoling her thus for her share in our family calamity.

❋

In my room awaiting my husband's return I mused alone. I remembered my brother. Try as I might, I could not see him as he is now, grown a man, dressed in American clothes, walking fearlessly about the strange roadways of that far country, speaking, perhaps, to its men and women—nay, certainly this, since one woman he loves. I could only look into my mind and remember him as I knew him best, the little elder brother of my childhood, he with whom I played at the threshold of the gates into the courts.

Then he was a head taller than I, quick to move, excited in speech, eager after laughter. His face was like our mother's, oval, its lips straight and fine, and the brows clearly marked above the pointed eyes. The older concubines were always jealous because he was more beautiful than their sons. Yet how could he be otherwise? They were but common women, slaves in their youth, their lips full and coarse, and their eyebrows scattered like dog's hairs. But our mother was a lady of a hundred generations. Her beauty was the beauty of precision and delicacy, full of restraint in line and color. This beauty she had bestowed upon her son.

Not that he cared for it. He brushed aside impatiently the caressing fingers of the women slaves upon his smooth cheeks, when they flattered him to try to please his mother. He was intent upon his own play. But indeed, he was intense even in play and laughter. I seem to see him always with knitted brows above his play. He was filled with resolution over everything, and he would brook no will over his own.

When we played together I dared not cross him, partly because he was a boy, and it would not have been seemly that I, a girl, should set my will against his. But I let him have his way most of all because I loved him greatly and could not see him grieve.

Indeed, no one could bear to see him crossed. The servants and the slaves revered him as the young lord, and even the dignity of our mother was softened in his presence. I do not mean that she ever allowed him actually to disobey her commands, but I think she often restrained herself so that what she commanded of him would be in accord with his wishes. I have heard her bid a slave remove a certain sweet oil cake from the table before he came in, because he loved it and would eat it, and it always made him ill; and lest seeing it he would desire it, and she be compelled to refuse it to him.

Even as a youth his life was thus made smooth before him. It did not occur to me to mark the difference made between him and me. I did not at any time dream of being on an equality with my brother. It was not necessary. I had no such important part to fulfill in the family as he, the first son and the heir of my father.

Always in those days I loved my brother above all others. I walked by his side in the gardens, clinging to his hand. Together we stooped above the shallow pools, searching in the green shadows for the particular goldfish we called our own. Together we collected little stones of varied colors and built fairy courts patterned after our own courts, only infinitely small and intricate in design. When he taught me to move my brush carefully over the outlined characters of my first writing book, guiding my hand with his own placed over it, I considered him the wisest of human beings. Wherever he went in the women's courts, I followed behind him like a little dog, and if he went beyond the arched gate into the men's apartments where I could not go, I stood patiently there waiting until he returned.

Then suddenly he was nine years old, and he was taken from the women's apartments into those of his father and the men, and our life together was broken sharply off.

Oh, those first few days! I could not live through them without long fits of weeping. At night I wept myself to sleep and dreamed of a place where we were always children and never separated. Ah, it was many a day before I ceased to mope about, seeing every room empty without him. My mother at length feared for my health and spoke to me.

"My daughter, this constant longing for your brother is unseemly. Such emotion must be reserved for other relationships. Grief like this is fit only for the death of your husband's parents. Perceive the proportions of life and restrain yourself, therefore. Apply yourself to your studies and to your embroidery. The time has now come when we must fit you seriously for your marriage."

Thereafter the idea of my approaching marriage was held always before me. I grew to understand that my life and my brother's could never go side by side. I did not belong primarily to his family, but to the family of my betrothed. I heeded my mother's words, therefore, and resolutely applied myself to my duties.

I remember my brother again clearly on that day when he desired to go to Peking to school. He came

into our mother's presence to ask her formal permission, and I was there. Since he had already obtained
our father's consent, his coming to our mother was
only a courtesy. Our mother could scarcely forbid
what our father allowed. But my brother was always
scrupulous in the observance of proper outward
custom.

He stood before her clad in a thin gray silk gown,
for it was summer. Upon his thumb was a ring of
jade. My brother is ever a lover of beautiful things.
That day he made me think of a silver reed for
grace. He held his head drooping a little before our
mother, his eyes cast down. But from where I sat I
could see his eyes gleaming between the lids.

"My mother," he said, "if you are willing, I
should like to study further at the university in
Peking."

She knew of course that she must consent. He
knew that she would have forbidden it if she could.
But where another would have dallied with com-
plaining and weeping, she spoke at once quietly
and firmly.

"My son, you know it must be as your father says.

I am nothing but your mother—I know it. Nevertheless, I will speak, even though I may not now command against your father's will. I see no use in your leaving home. Your father and your grandfather completed their learning at home. You yourself have had the most skilled scholars in the city to teach you from your childhood. We even procured T'ang, the Learned, from Szechuen to instruct you in poetry. This foreign learning is unnecessary for one in your position. Going to these far cities you imperil your life, which is not fully yours until you have given us a son to carry on the ancestral name. If you could have married first—"

My brother stirred angrily and shut his fan, which he had been holding open in his left hand. Then he opened it quickly again with a snap. He lifted his eyes, and from under their lids protest leaped out. My mother raised her hand.

"Do not speak, my son. I do not command yet. I only warn you. Your life is not your own. Take care of it."

She bowed her head, and he was dismissed.

I saw him after that but rarely. He came home

only twice before my marriage, and we had nothing
to say to each other, and we were never alone together. Nearly always he came into the women's
courts merely to give his mother formal greeting or
to bid her farewell, and I could not speak to him
freely in the presence of an elder.

I saw only that he grew tall and erect in bearing,
and his face lost some of its youthful delicacy. He
lost, too, the slender, childish, drooping grace of his
body that in his early years had given him the look
almost of a handsome girl. I heard him tell my
mother that in the foreign type of school he had to
exercise his body daily, and thus it grew in height
and thickness and sinew. His hair he cut off according to the new fashion at the time of the first revolution, and it was smooth and black against his lifted
head. I saw that he was beautiful. The women in the
courts sighed after him, and the fat Second Lady
murmured,

"Ah, he is like his father when first we loved!"

Then my brother went across the seas, and I did
not see him again. He became indistinct in my mind
and dimmed by all the strangeness surrounding him,
so that I have never again seen him clearly.

Sitting in my room, awaiting my husband's return, with the letter from my mother in my hand, I perceived that my brother was a strange man whom I did not know.

When my husband came home at noon I ran to him weeping, the letter in my outstretched hands. He received me with surprise, saying,

"But what is this? But what is this?"

"Read this—read and see!" I cried, and fell to sobbing afresh to see the look on his face as he read.

"Stupid boy—foolish—foolish!" he muttered, crumpling the letter in his hand. "How could he do this thing? Yes, go at once to your honorable mother. You must comfort her."

And he bade the servant tell the ricksha man to hasten his meal that I might lose no time. When the man was ready then, I took only the child and his attendant and besought the man to run quickly.

When I had entered the gate of my mother's house I perceived at once the silence of heaviness over all, as a cloud dims the moon. The slaves went about their business rolling their eyes and whispering, and Wang Da Ma, who had returned with me, had wept as we passed through the streets until her eyelids were thickened with tears.

In the Court of the Drooping Willows, the Second and the Third Ladies sat with their children. When I entered with my son they could scarce give me greeting before they fell to questioning me eagerly.

"Ah, the fair child!" cried the plump Second Lady, laying her pretty fat fingers against my son's cheek and smelling his little hand in caress. "A little sweetmeat, thou!— Have you heard?" She turned to me with important gravity.

I nodded. I asked,

"Where is my mother?"

"The Honorable First Lady has remained in her chamber these three days," she replied. "She speaks to no one. There she sits in her chamber. Twice daily she comes forth into the outer room to command the ordering of the household and to give out rice and food. Then she returns again to her chamber. Her lips are set together like the lips of a stone image, and her eyes make us turn away. We dare not speak to her. We do not know her thoughts.

"You will tell us what she says to you?" She coaxed me with nods and smiles, but I shook my head, refusing her curiosity. "At least leave us the little precious to play with," she added.

She stretched out her arms for my son, but I forbade it.

"I will take him to my mother," I said. "He will cheer her and turn her mind outward from her distress."

When I had passed through the guest hall into the Court of Peonies and then through the women's leisure room, I paused before my mother's apartments. Usually only the red satin curtain hung in this doorway, but now behind the curtain the door was closed. Then I struck lightly upon it with the palm of my hand. There was no answer. I struck again. It was only when I called,

"It is I, my mother! It is I, thy little child!" that I heard her voice coming as from a great distance,

"Come to me, my daughter."

Then I went in. I saw her sitting beside the black carved table. Incense was smoldering in the bronze urn before the sacred writing on the wall. She sat with bowed head, and between the fingers of one drooping hand she held a book. When she saw me enter she said,

"You have come? I have been trying to read the Book of Changes. But I find nothing to-day in its pages to comfort me." She shook her head a little vaguely as she spoke, and the book dropped upon the floor. She let it lie there.

The irresolution of the action alarmed me. My mother has ever been self-possessed, sure, restrained. Now I saw that she had been too long alone, I reproached myself that I had loved my son too well and that his father's tenderness had comforted me too deeply and too long. It had been many days since I came to visit her. How could I rouse her and divert her thoughts? I took my son and placing him on his fat legs, I folded his little hands and made him bow before her. I whispered to him,

"Thy honored Old One—say it, child!"

"Old One!" he lisped, staring at her unsmiling.

I told you that she had not seen him since his third month, and you know, My Sister, how he is altogether beautiful! Who could resist him? Her eyes fell on him and lingered. She roused herself. She went to the gilded cupboard and took out a red lacquered box. She opened it, and within were tiny cakes covered with sesame seed. These she gave to him, filling his hands. When he saw them he laughed aloud, and she indulged him with faint smiles and said.

"Eat, my little lotus-pod! Eat, my little meat-dumpling!"

Seeing her thus momentarily diverted, I picked up the book and poured a bowl of tea from the pot on the table, and presented it to her in both my hands.

She bade me sit, then, and the child played upon the floor, and we watched him. I waited for her to speak, not knowing whether or not she wished to mention the matter of my brother. She did not immediately approach it. She said first,

"Your son is here, my daughter."

I remembered then the night when I had told her of my grief. Now the joy of the morning had come.

"Yes, my mother," I replied, smiling.

"You are happy?" she asked, her eyes still on the child.

"My lord is a prince for his grace to me, his humble wife," I replied.

"The child is conceived and born as from perfection," she said musingly, her eyes upon him. "In everything I observe he is ten parts and complete. There is no beauty left to desire in him. Ah—" She sighed and stirred restlessly. "Your brother was such a child! I wish that he had died then, that I might have remembered him as beautiful and filial!"

I understood therefore that she wished to speak of my brother. But I waited to perceive the direction of her thoughts more clearly. In a little while she spoke again, raising her eyes to mine,

"You had my letter?"

"My mother's letter reached me this morning by the hand of the servant," I replied, bowing.

She sighed again, and rising, she went to the drawer of the writing-table and drew forth yet another letter. I stood and awaited her return. When she gave me the letter I received it with both hands. She said,

"Read it."

It was from a friend of my brother's, surnamed

Chu, with whom he had gone to America from Peking. At the request of my brother, the letter said, he, Chu Kwoh-ting, was writing to the honored Old Ones to tell them that their son had betrothed himself according to the western custom to the daughter of one of his teachers in the university. He, their son, sent his filial respects to his parents and begged them to break off the early betrothal with the daughter of Li, which had always made him unhappy, even in contemplation. He acknowledged in all things the superior virtue of his parents and their endless kindness to him, their unworthy son. Nevertheless he wished to say clearly that he could not marry the one to whom he had been betrothed according to Chinese custom, because the times had changed; he was a modern man, and he had decided to adopt the modern, independent, free method of marriage.

The letter closed with many formal and filial expressions of respectful affection and obedience. But none the less the determination in my brother's heart was written plainly forth. He had asked his friend to write for him only because he wished to spare his parents and himself the embarrassment of direct defiance. My heart burned against him as I read the letter. When I had finished it I folded it and handed it back to my mother without speech.

"He is seized with a madness," said my mother. "I have sent him the electric letter to command his instant return."

Then I knew how great was her agitation. For my mother is altogether of the old China. When in the streets of our ancient and beautiful city tall poles were reared which carried wires as the branches of a tree may carry spiders' webs, she had cried out against the desecration.

"Our ancients used the brush and the ink block, and what have we, their unworthy descendants, to say of greater importance than their august words, that we need such speed?" she said in indignation.

And when she heard that words could travel even under the sea itself, she said,

"And what is there that we wish to communicate to these barbarians? Did not the gods in their wisdom pour out the sea between us in order to separate us from them? It is impious to unite what the gods in their wisdom have put apart."

But now such need for haste had come even to her!

"I had thought," she said sadly, "that I should never use these foreign inventions. Nor should I, had my son remained in his own country. But when one deals with the barbarians, one must harness the very devil to one's mill!"

I spoke then to soothe her.

"My mother, do not grieve overmuch. My brother is obedient. He will listen and turn from this folly of running after a foreign woman."

But she shook her head. She leaned her brow upon her hands. A sudden anxiety fell upon me to see it. She was looking really ill! She had never been full-fleshed, but now she was wasted away, and her hand, supporting her head, trembled. I leaned forward to observe her with more care, when she began to speak slowly.

"I have learned long ago," she said, her voice coming faintly and with great weariness, "that when a woman has crawled into a man's heart, his eyes are fastened inward upon her so that he is blind for a space to anything else." She paused to rest, and then went on, her words coming at last like sighs. "Your father—is he not accounted an honorable man? Yet have I long resigned myself to this thing; when a woman's beauty seizes him and catches his desire, he is mad for a time and understands nothing reasonable. And he has known a score of singing girls, beside these idle mouths he brings home as concubines—three of them we have had, and the only reason we have not another is because his lust failed for the Peking girl before the negotiations were finished. How then can the son show greater wisdom than the father?

"Men!" She roused herself suddenly. She curled her lips until her mouth seemed a thing alive of its own scorn. "Their inner thoughts are always coiled like snakes about the living body of some woman!"

I sat in horror at her words. Never had she spoken before of my father and the concubines. I saw suddenly into the inner halls of her heart. The bitterness and suffering there were bowels of fire within her. I had no words wherewith to comfort her—I, the beloved of my husband. I tried to imagine his taking a Second Lady. I could not. I could only remember the hours of our love, and my involuntary eyes fell upon our son, playing still with the little sesame cakes. What had I to say of comfort to my mother?

Yet I longed to speak.

"It may be that the foreign woman—" I began timidly.

But she struck her long pipe upon the floor. She had just taken it from the table and had begun to fill it with hasty, trembling fingers.

"Let us have no talk about that one," she said sharply. "I have spoken. Now it is for my son to obey. He shall return and marry the daughter of Li, his betrothed, and of her shall his first seed come. Thus can his duty be fulfilled to the Ancient Ones. Then he may take whom he likes for a small wife! Shall I expect the son to be more perfect than the father?—But be silent now and leave me. I am very tired. I must rest awhile upon my bed."

I could say no more. I saw indeed that she was

very pale, and that her body drooped like a withered reed. I took up my son, therefore, and withdrew from her presence.

❋

When I had returned to my home I told my husband with tears that I had not been able to soften the sorrow of my mother. He comforted me with his hand upon my hand, and bade me wait with patience the coming of my brother. When he talked gently with me thus, I took hope for the future. But the next morning when he was gone to his work I fell into doubt again. I cannot forget my mother!

Out of the sadness of her life these many years she has had this great hope of the future—the hope of all good women; she has thought of her son's son to stay her old age, to fulfill her duty to the family. How is it that my brother has placed his careless desire before his mother's life? I shall reproach my brother. I will tell him all that my mother said. I will remind him that he is my mother's only son. Then I will say,

"How can you place upon our mother's knees the child of a foreigner?"

✻✻✻✻✻✻✻✻✻✻✻✻✻✻✻✻✻✻

XI

WE have heard nothing yet, My Sister! Every day
I send the gardener to my mother's house to inquire
of her health and to know whether or not word
has come of my brother. Every day now for fifteen
days he answers,

"The Honorable Old One says she is not ill, but
to the eyes of her servants she wastes. She cannot
eat. As for the young lord, there is no word. Doubt-
less for this reason her heart is eating her body. At
her age anxiety cannot be easily endured."

"Oh, why does not my brother send word? I have
prepared delicate food for my mother and set it in
fine porcelain bowls; I have sent it by the hands of
servants and I have said,

"Eat of this poor meat, my mother. It is tasteless,
but because these hands have prepared it, deign to
eat a little."

They tell me she begins to eat, and then she puts
down her chopsticks. She cannot release her heart

[145]

of its anxiety. Is my brother then to be allowed to
kill my mother? He should know that she cannot
endure the unfilial ways of the West. It is shameful
that he does not remember his duty!

I spend many hours meditating and wondering.
I cannot decide what my brother will do. At first
I did not question his final obedience to our mother.
Are not his body and his skin and his hair derived
from her? Can he therefore contaminate this sacred-
ness with a foreigner?

Moreover, my brother has been taught from his
first youth that wisdom of the Great Master which
says, "The first duty of a man is to pay careful heed
to every desire of his parents." When my father
returns and hears what my brother is about to do,
surely he also will forbid it. I persuaded myself
therefore into calm.

Thus I reasoned at first. But to-day I am as a
stream unsettled and shifting its waters upon the
sands beneath it.

My husband, My Sister, he it is who makes me
doubt the wisdom of the old ways. By the hold of

love upon me he makes me doubt! Last night he said strange things. I will tell you; it was like this—

We sat upon the little brick terrace he has had placed to the south of the house. Our son was asleep upstairs in his bamboo bed. The servants had withdrawn to their own affairs, I sat upon the porcelain garden seat a little apart from my lord, as was fitting. He lay in a long reed chair.

Together we watched the full-faced moon, swinging high in the heavens. The night wind had sprung up, and across the sky a procession of white clouds whirled with the speed of great snowy birds, now obscuring, now leaving magically clear, the face of the moon. So swift were the clouds that it was as if the moon itself were spinning above the trees. The smell of rain clung to the night air. Delight in this beauty and peace welled up within me. I was suddenly greatly content with my life. I raised my eyes, and I saw that my husband gazed at me. Exquisite and shy pleasure trembled in me.

"Such a moon!" he said at last, his voice moved with his own content. "Will you play the old harp, Kwei-lan?"

I teased him with mock reproach.

"The harp has six abhorrences and seven prohibitions, according to our ancients who made it," I said. "It will not give forth its voice in the presence of mourning, in the presence of festive instruments, when the musician is unhappy, when his person is defiled, when incense has not been freshly lighted, or when in the presence of an unsympathetic listener. If it will not sing to-night, my lord, which of these abhorrences is present?"

He became grave then, saying,

"No, my heart; I know that once it would not give forth its voice because I was that abhorrence, an unsympathetic listener, But now? Let your fingers sing the old songs of love, the songs of the poets."

Then did I rise and fetch my harp, and laying it upon the little stone table beside him, I stood and touched its strings while I meditated what to sing to him. At last I sang thus,

> "Cool is the autumn wind,
> Clear is the autumn moon.
> The dead leaves fall and scatter again;
> A raven, frost-smitten, starts from the tree.
> Where are you, Beloved?

Shall I meet you once more?
Ah, my heart weeps to-night—
I am alone!"

Then did this sad refrain echo again and again
from the strings, long after my fingers ceased to
touch them. "—Alone—Alone—Alone—" The wind
caught the echo, and suddenly the garden was full
of the mournful sound. It vibrated in me strangely
and called up my sadness which had rested forgotten
for an hour. It was the sadness of my mother. I
laid my hands softly upon the strings to cease their
moaning. I said,

"It is I, my lord, who am the abhorrence to-night.
I am grieved, I, the musician, and the harp moans
on of its own accord."

"Grieved?" He rose, and coming to me he took
my hand.

"It is my mother," I said faintly, daring to rest my
head for an instant against his arm. "She grieves, and
her grief speaks to me through the harp. It is my
brother. I feel the restlessness in her this night.
Everything is restless, waiting for his coming. She
has no one now except him. It is long since there

[149]

was anything between my father and her, and even I am of another family now—yours."

My husband said nothing at first. He took from his pocket a foreign-tobacco and lit it. He spoke at last in a calm voice.

"You must be prepared," he said. "It is better to face the truth. He will probably not obey your mother."

I was alarmed.

"Oh, why do you think this?" I asked.

"Why do you think he will?" he questioned in return, puffing out lengths of tobacco smoke from his mouth.

I drew away from him.

"No, do not reply with questions. I do not know —I am not clever, and never at reasons! If I have a real reason it is that he has been taught to know obedience to parents as the foundation of the state, and a son's duty—"

"Old foundations are breaking—have broken." He interrupted me with a significant look. "There must be stronger reasons than that in these days!"

I was filled with doubt as he spoke. Then I re-membered a secret comfort of my own—a thing I had not spoken aloud. This was my inner thought.

"But foreign women are so ugly," I whispered. "How shall a man of our race marry among them? Their own men have no recourse, but—"

I fell silent, for I was ashamed to speak of men thus before my husband. Yet how could a man desire such women as that one we had seen before my son's birth? Such light flat eyes and faded hair, such coarse hands and feet? I knew my brother! Was he not the son of my father, and had not my father ever loved above all things in the world beauty in women?

But my husband laughed shortly.

"Ha! Not all Chinese women are beautiful, and not all foreign women are ugly! The daughter of Li, to whom your brother is betrothed, is not a beauty, I hear. They say in the tea-shops that her lips are too wide—that they are curved downward like a rice-sickle—"

"What have the idlers of the tea-shops to do, speaking of such a thing?" I cried in indignation. "She is a respectable maiden, and her family is noble!"

He shrugged his shoulders.

"I only mention what I hear and what your

[151]

brother must have heard," he replied. "It may be that such talk has made it more easy to fix his wandering heart upon another woman."

We were silent an instant.

"And these foreign women!" he continued, smoking and musing. "Some of them are like the White Star for beauty! Clear eyes—free bodies—"

I turned, and I opened my eyes wide at my husband. But he did not see me. He went on,

"Those beautiful, bare arms of theirs—they have none of the artificial modesties and the reserves of our women, I can tell you. They are free as the sun and the wind are free; with laughter and dancing they pluck out a man's heart and let it run through their fingers like sunlight, to waste upon the ground."

My breath ceased for a moment. Of whom did he speak then, my husband? What foreigner had taught him thus? I felt a sudden bitter anger rising in me.

"You—you have—" I faltered.

But he shook his head, laughing a little at me.

"What a woman you are! No—none ever wasted my heart thus. I kept it somehow until—" His tone dropped into tenderness, and my heart recognized it, and I was eased.

"But it was hard?" I whispered.

"Well, yes, sometimes. We Chinese men have been kept so separate. Our women are reserved, demure. They reveal nothing. And to a young man —and your brother is young—these others, these foreign women, with their beautiful, swan-white flesh, their exquisite bodies offering themselves in the dance—"

"Hush, my lord," I said with dignity. "This is men's talk. I will not hear it. Are these people really as uncultivated and savage as this sounds on your lips?"

"No," he replied slowly. "It is partly because their nation is young, and youth takes its pleasures in crude form. But I speak of this because your brother is young, too. And even if you do not like to hear it, yet it is not to be forgotten that the lips of his betrothed are wide and curved like a rice-sickle." He smiled again, and seating himself he fell to staring at the moon.

My husband is wise. I cannot lightly cast aside his

words. From what he has said I begin to perceive that there is some transient charm about the uncovered flesh of these foreign women. Hearing him speak, I am disturbed by it. It makes me remember the glittering eyes and the laughter of my father and his favorite concubine. I shudder, and yet I cannot draw my thoughts away.

I pondered, therefore. It is true that my brother is a man. Moreover, his continued silence is an evil sign. It has ever been his way from childhood to let silence deepen with determination. As a babe if our mother forbade him something, Wang Da Ma said he would grow suddenly silent and seize the thing yet more firmly.

I placed the harp in its lacquered case at last with a sigh. The moon had yielded itself to the clouds utterly, and a light rain began to fall. The night's mood changed; we went into the house. I slept ill.

✻✻✻✻✻✻✻✻✻✻✻✻✻✻✻✻✻✻

XII

THE dawn came this day under a still, gray sky. *10*
The air is heavy with late heat and full of damp-
ness. The child frets, although I can find no sick-
ness in him.

The servant returning to-day from his inquiry at
my mother's house brought word that my father
has come. It seems that Wang Da Ma took courage
to send him a letter through the professional letter-
writer who sits at the temple gate, begging humbly
that he come because my mother's strength does not
increase. Day after day she sits in her chamber. She
cannot eat. My father, receiving the letter, has come
home for two days.

I determined, therefore, to go to see him. I dressed
my son in red. It is the first time my father has seen
him.

I found my father seated by the pool in the Court
of the Goldfish. Since the air was hot, and since he

EAST WIND: WEST WIND

is now exceedingly fat, he sat beside the pool clad
only in his inner coat and trousers of summer silk,
pale as the water under the willows. The Second
Lady stood beside him fanning him, although the
perspiration rolled down her own cheeks from the
unaccustomed exertion; and on his knees sat one of
his children in gala dress for his return.

When I entered the court he clapped his hands
and cried,

"Aha—aha—here comes the mother and her son!"

He set his child from his knee and bade my son
approach, enticing him in a low voice and with
smiles. I bowed deeply and he nodded, his eyes still
fixed on my son. Then I folded my son's hands and
bade him bow. My father was greatly pleased.

"Aha—aha—" he kept repeating softly. He lifted
my son to his knee and felt his round arms and legs,
and laughed at his wide, astonished eyes.

"Such a man!" he cried in delight. "Let a slave
bring sweetmeats for him! Let the candied persimmons be brought, and the little larded cakes!"

I was dismayed. My child has but ten teeth at best.
How then could he eat candied persimmons?

"O my honored father!" I begged. "Consider his

[156]

tender years. His little stomach is used only to soft food. I beg you—"

But my father waved his hand to silence me and talked to the child. I was compelled to submit.

"But you are a man! And does your mother still feed you on pap? My daughter, I have had sons also—many sons, four or five?—I cannot remember. At any rate, I know more about sons than the mother of only one, even of such an one!" He rumbled a great laugh and continued, "Ah, if my son, your brother, but breeds me such a one as this by the daughter of Li to worship my old bones!"

Since he had mentioned my brother I was emboldened to ask,

"But if he weds a foreigner, my father? It is this fear which wastes away my mother's heart until she is day by day weaker in body."

"Pst! He cannot," he replied lightly. "How can he wed without my consent? It is not legal. Your mother is needlessly agitated over this whole affair. I have said to her this very morning,

" 'Cease your foolish fretting. Let the lad play with his foreigner. He is twenty-four years old, and his blood urges him. It is nothing. At his age I had three

singing girls whom I loved. Let him have his
pleasure. When he wearies of her—say, in two
moons or, if she be really a beauty, in four or five,
perhaps, although I do not expect that—he will set-
tle the more readily to his marriage. Can it be supposed that he will live a monk for four years, even
though he is in a foreign country? Are not foreign
women yet women?'

"But your mother has ever been incomprehensible.
From the very first she has been possessed by some
strange intensity. Nay, I do not speak ill of her. She
is wise, and under her hands my gold and silver is
not carelessly spent. I do not complain. She never
lashes about me with her tongue as some women do.
There are times when I wish she would, so that I be
not met with this silence that baffled me even in the
beginning. Oh, it is nothing now—it does not matter.
No one understands the caprices of women. But
since her youth she has had this fault, a gravity too
intense for ease in daily life. She seizes upon some
thought, some imagined duty, and then that becomes
life itself to her. It is very trying—"

He broke off his speech in an irritation I had never
seen in him before. He took the fan from the hand

of the Second Lady and began fanning himself
sharply. He set my son on the ground and seemed to
forget him. He went on almost in anger,

"And now she has some strange woman's fancy
that our son's first union should produce a grandson
for us—a superstitious idea that the child will there-
by be more gifted of heaven. Ah, women are willful!
And the best of them are ignorant, having been shut
away from the world."

He closed his eyes and fanned himself in silence
for a few moments, and his irritation passed away.
His usual look of peaceful, smiling good humor
came over his face. He opened his eyes and pressed
cakes upon my son, saying,

"Eat, my little one! What does it all matter? Do
not fret yourself, my daughter. Can a son disobey his
father and live? I cannot be troubled."

Still was I not content, and after a silence, I had
more that must be spoken.

"But, my father, if he refuse to marry his betrothed? I have heard that in these changed times—"

But my father would have none of it. He waved
his hand lightly and smiled.

"Refuse? I have not heard anywhere that a son

may refuse his father. Calm yourself, my daughter. A year from now he will have begot a son according to the law, by the daughter of Li. Such a one as thou, my little man!"

And he patted my son's cheek.

※

I told my husband what my father had said, and he heard and replied thoughtfully,

"The trouble in all this may be that the foreigner is not willing to accept a subordinate position. It is not customary in their country for men to have secondary wives."

I had nothing to say in immediate answer. It had not occurred to me to think of her or what she would think of our customs. Had she not succeeded in enticing my brother? What more then could she desire? I had thought thus far only of my brother and of his duty to his parents.

"You mean she would expect to be my brother's only wife all her days?" I asked.

I was even a little indignant. How could she expect to forbid my brother what was his legal right according to the law of his country? How could she demand more of him than my honored mother had demanded of my father? I told my husband this.

"It is very simple, I think," I said in conclusion. "If she marries a man of our race, she must give him the freedom to which he is accustomed. She cannot bring her foreign ways here."

My husband looked at me and smiled most curiously. I could not understand him. Then he spoke,

"Suppose I said that I wished to take a small wife —a concubine?"

Something cold smote me like snow thrust into my bare bosom. I whispered,

"Oh, no, my lord—you never could—not now! I have given you a son!"

He leaped to his feet, and I felt his arm about my shoulders. He was murmuring,

"No, no, my little heart—I do not mean that—I would not—could not, indeed—"

But his other words had been too sudden. They are the words which many a wife fears and even expects, but I had not, since he loved me. Now without warning he had driven into my heart all the anguish of my mother and the anguish of a hundred generations of women who loved their lords and lost their favor. I fell to sudden weeping that I could not control.

Then my husband comforted me, holding my hands and murmuring—but I cannot tell you his words, My Sister. Spoken again even between us they would shame me. I am made shy when I think of them. They were love made most exquisite. My weeping stilled itself, and I was comforted.

When we had been silent a space he asked me,

"But why did you weep?"

I hung my head, and I felt the quick blood leap into my cheeks. He raised my head in his hands.

"Why—why?" he persisted, and as ever in answer to his questions, truth came to my lips.

"Because my lord dwells in my heart," I faltered, "and fills it utterly and I would—"

My voice fell of its own accord into silence, but his eyes answered. Then he said in a low voice and most tenderly,

"And what if she loves your brother thus? Her nature does not differ from the nature of all women because she happens to be born over the western seas. You are women, and you are alike in your spirit and your desires."

I had not thought of her like this. I see that I have understood nothing clearly. It is ever my husband who teaches me.

"Oh, I am afraid—afraid! I begin to understand a little now. What shall we do if there is this love between the foreign one and my brother?"

❋❋❋❋❋❋❋❋❋❋❋❋❋❋❋❋❋❋

XIII

A LETTER has come from my brother! He has written a letter to me and to my husband, pleading for
our help. He beseeches me to intercede with our
parents for him. And then he speaks of her—of the
foreigner! He uses lightning words to tell of her
beauty. He says she is like a pine tree covered with
snow for great beauty.

And then, O My Sister, then he says that he is
already married to her according to the law of her
country! He is bringing her home, now that he has
received our mother's letter demanding his presence.
He pleads as for his very life that we will help them
—because they love each other!

I am undone. Because of what lives between my
husband and me I am undone utterly. I cannot hear
my mother speak now. I do not remember her sadness. I do not remember that my brother has disobeyed her. By nothing else than this could my

brother have persuaded me; if she loves him as I love my lord, how can I refuse them anything?

I will go to my mother.

Three days have now passed, My Sister, since I approached my mother. I prepared myself to enter her presence with humbleness. I chose my words previously as a bridegroom chooses jewels for his bride. I went into her room alone, and I stood before her. I spoke delicately, beseeching her.

She understood nothing—nothing, My Sister! We are estranged, my mother and I. She accuses me silently of befriending the foreigner and of taking my brother's part against his mother. Although she does not say this, I know in her heart she speaks thus to herself. She will hear nothing of my explanations.

This, though I had planned my speech with all care! I said in my heart,

"I will awaken in her memories of her own marriage and of those first days of my father's love, when she was at the time of her own great beauty and youth."

But how can such stiff and formal molds as words contain the spirit-essence of love? It is as if one tried to imprison a rosy cloud within an iron vessel. It is like painting butterflies with a harsh brush of bamboo. When I spoke, hesitating because of its delicacy, of this spell of love between the young, of that secret harmony binding one heart unexpectedly to another, she grew scornful.

"There is no such thing as this between man and woman," she said haughtily. "It is only desire. Do not use poetical expressions in regard to it. It is only desire—the man's desire for the woman, the woman's desire for a son. When that desire is satisfied, there is nothing left."

I tried afresh.

"Do you remember, my mother, when you and my father were wed, how your spirits spoke?"

But she struck her thin hot fingers against my lips.

"Do not speak of him. In his heart there have been a hundred women. To which one does his spirit speak?"

"And your heart, my mother?" I asked softly, taking her hand. It lay in my hand, quivering, and then she withdrew it.

"It is empty," she said. "It awaits my grandson, the son of my son. When he shall have been taken before the tablets of his ancestors, I may die in peace."

She turned away from me and refused to speak further.

I came away sad. What has separated me so far from my mother? We cry aloud, but we do not hear each other. We speak, but we do not understand each other. I feel I am changed, and I know I am changed by love.

I am like a frail bridge, spanning the infinity between past and present. I clasp my mother's hand; I cannot let it go, for without me she is alone. But my husband's hand holds mine; his hand holds mine fast. I can never let love go!

What of the future then, My Sister?

I pass my days in waiting. I seem to dream, and the dream is always of blue water and upon it a white ship. It is speeding like a great bird for the shore. If I could, I would stretch out my hand to mid-ocean and seize that ship and hold it there that it might never come. How else can my brother be happy in what he has done? There is no place for him now in his home under his father's roof.

But my feeble hands can stop nothing. I only dream, and I can think of nothing clearly. Nothing can make the ship seem remote except my son, smiling and babbling his first words. I keep him beside me all day. But at night I wake up, and I hear the thunder of the waves about me. Hour by hour the ship rushes on, and nothing can stay it from coming nearer.

What will it be like when my brother comes, bringing her? I fear such strangeness. I am dumb in this time of waiting. I know neither good nor ill, only waiting.

Seven days, my husband says, and the white ship will reach the harbor at the mouth of the river, the great Son of the Sea, which flows past the North gate of the city. My husband cannot understand why I cling to the hours to stretch them longer and put further into the future the eighth day. I cannot put into words for him my fear of this strangeness to come.

He is a man. How can he understand the heart of my mother? I cannot forget how she dreads my brother's coming. I have not been to see her again. We have nothing now to say to each other. Only I cannot forget her and that she is alone.

Yet I cannot forget either my brother and that one whom he loves. I am torn hither and thither like a frail plum-tree in a wind too passionate for its resistance.

❀❀❀❀❀❀❀❀❀❀❀❀❀❀❀❀❀

XIV

I COULD not wait for your leisure, My Sister! I have come afoot. I have left my son, thrusting him into his nurse's arms, regardless of his screams when he saw me departing. No—no tea! I must return immediately. I ran only to tell you—

They have come! My brother and the foreign one, they have come! They came two hours ago and they have eaten with us. I have seen her. I have heard her speak, but I can understand nothing she says. She is so strange that I stare at her even against my will.

They came in as we sat at breakfast. The gate-man rushed into our presence, and scarcely stopping to bow he gasped,

"There is a man at the gate with a person whose like I have not seen! I do not know even whether it is male or female. It is tall like a man, and yet the face has the look of a woman's face!"

My husband looked at me and laid his chopsticks down.

"It is they," he said quietly in answer to my astonished eyes.

He went to the gate himself then, and immediately they entered the house. I stood to greet them, and when I saw the tall, foreign figure, speech dried in my mouth. I scarcely saw my brother at all. I was conscious only of her, the foreigner, of her height, slender in some dark blue robe that fell straight below her knees.

But my husband was not confused at all. He bade them be seated at the table with us, and he ordered fresh tea and rice. I said nothing. I could only look at her and look at her again.

Even now I can only say over and over again, "What shall we do with this strange woman? How can she ever belong in our life?"

I do not remember that my brother loves her. I am confused with astonishment at her presence here in my house. It is like a dream which, even while one dreams, seems untrue and soon to pass, because it is too unreal.

You ask what she is like? I scarcely know how to tell you, although, as I said, I have done nothing but stare at her since she entered the door. Let me think what she is like.

She is taller than my brother. Her head is shorn. Yet her hair does not lie decorously about her ears; it is as if blown by the four winds, and it is tawny, the color of tiger-bone wine. Her eyes are like the sea under a stormy sky, and she does not smile easily.

At once I asked myself when I saw her, is she beautiful? But I answer, she is not beautiful. Her eyebrows are not delicate and moth-like, as we love to see a woman's brows. They are dark and heavily marked above her brooding eyes. Beside hers, my brother's face appears youthful, with rounded flesh and slighter bones. Yet she is only twenty—four years younger than he.

As for her hands, were her hands placed beside my brother's and their bodies concealed, I would say his were the woman's hands. His are soft with olive flesh. The bones of her hands protrude beneath the skin, and her wrists are much coarser than mine.

When she grasped my hand I felt her palm was knotted and hard against mine. I mentioned it to my husband after breakfast when we were an instant alone. He said it is because of a game called tennis, which these foreign women play with their men— I suppose, to amuse them. How strangely do the foreign women woo love!

Her feet are longer by two inches than my brother's feet—at least, it so appears. How embarrassing this must be to them both!

As for my brother, he is dressed in western clothes, and he is foreign to me in many ways. He moves quickly, and he is restless. When I look at him I cannot see anywhere the silvery, drooping youth he once was. Now his head is erect, and when he is not speaking his face is unsmiling. He wears no rings or ornaments of any kind, except a plain gold ring upon one hand on the third finger. This ring has not even a jewel of any kind set into it. The rigid dark clothes of the West mark more clearly his pallor.

Even when he sits, it is as foreigners sit, with one knee placed over the other. He speaks without effort

the foreign language to my husband and to her, and
the words roll from their mouths with a clatter like
that of pebbles against a rock.

He is altogether changed. Even his eyes are
changed. They are no longer cast down. They are
swift and fearless, and they look boldly at the person
to whom he speaks. He wears spectacles made curiously of gold and some sort of dark shell, and they
make him in appearance older than he is.

But his lips are still the lips of our mother, thin,
delicate, pressed together in repose. Only on my
brother's lips there hangs yet a trace of the old childish sullenness that always came when he was refused
a desire. By this I knew my brother.

I and my son, we are the only Chinese among us,
I think. They stand there in our house, wrapped in
their strange dress, talking their strange tongue to
each other. I and my son, we do not understand
them.

They are to stay at our house until our father and
our mother receive them. When it is known to my
mother that I have allowed them to dwell here, she
will be incensed at my unfilial roof. I tremble. Yet

as my husband wishes, so it must be. And after all, is this not my brother, the son of one mother with me?

When we sit down to rice all together, she cannot eat with the chopsticks. I laugh secretly behind my sleeve because she cannot hold them even as well as my son holds them in his tiny hands. She grasps them firmly, and her brows knit themselves in her earnest endeavor to learn. But her hands are un-skilled in delicate things. She knows nothing.

Her voice, My Sister, is not like any woman's voice that I have heard. We like to hear a woman's voice light and soft, like a small stream of water trickling between two rocks, or like the piping of little birds in the reeds. But her voice is deep and full, and since she speaks but seldom, one pauses to listen to it. It has the rich note of the voice of the harvest thrush in spring, when the rice is waiting to be cut into sheaves. When she speaks, her words fall in rapid phrases to my brother, to my husband. She does not speak to me for we do not understand each other.

Twice she has smiled, a quick, shining smile, springing up out of her eyes like a silver flash of sunshine on a sullen stream. When she smiles I understand her. She says, "Shall we be friends?" We look at each other doubtfully.

Then I answer silently, "When you see my son I shall know whether or not we can be friends."

I dressed my son in his red silk coat and his green trousers. I placed upon his feet the cherry blossom embroidered shoes. Upon his head I placed his round crownless hat with the circle of tiny gold Buddhas about it, and on his neck I put a silver chain.

When he was garbed thus, he looked a very princeling, and I brought him to her. He stood before her on widespread legs and stared at her astonished. I bade him bow, and he placed his little hands together and bowed, staggering with his effort.

She gazed at him smiling. When he bowed she laughed aloud, a low laugh like a note struck from a deep bell, and then crying a sweet, unknown word, she seized him and held him against her and placed her lips upon his soft neck. His hat dropped off

and from over his shaven head she looked at me.
Such a look, My Sister! Her eyes said,
"I desire one exactly like him!"
I smiled, saying, "Then we shall be friends!"
I think I begin to see why my brother loves her.

Now the fifth day has passed since their coming.
They have not yet presented themselves before my
father and my mother. My husband and my brother
spend hours together in troubled talk in the foreign
tongue. I do not know what they have concluded.
Whatever is done must be done slowly. Meanwhile,
I watch the foreign one.

If you ask me what I think of her, My Sister, I do
not know. Certainly she is not like our women.
Every movement of her body is free and unrestrained and full of a rapid grace. Her gaze is direct
and unafraid. Her eyes seek the eyes of my brother
without shyness. She listens to the men speak, and
then she throws into their talk a quick word, and
they laugh. She is accustomed to men, as the Fourth
Lady was.

And yet there is a difference between them. The Fourth Lady, it seemed to me, beneath the assurance of her beauty in the presence of men yet had fear. I think it was because she was afraid, even at the height of her loveliness, of the moment when it would begin to slip away from her and she would have nothing left wherewith to draw the hearts of men to her.

This foreign one has no fear of anything in her, although she is not beautiful as the Fourth Lady was beautiful. She does not trouble herself. She accepts as her right the interest of men. She makes no effort to win their glances. She seems to say, "This is I. I am as you see me. I do not care to be otherwise."

I think she is very proud. At least she seems strangely indifferent to the difficulties she has brought into our family. She plays idly with my son, she reads books—she brought with her her many boxes of books—she writes letters. Such letters! I gazed over her shoulder, and the page was covered with large, sprawling marks, hooked each to the other. I could make nothing of any of it. But most of all she likes to sit in the garden dreaming, doing nothing at all. I have not once seen any embroidery in her hands.

One day she and my brother went out together early in the morning and returned at noon, dusty and earth-soiled. I asked my husband in great surprise where they had been to come back in such a condition. He replied,

"They have been for what westerners call 'hike.'"

"What is this 'hike'?" I asked, greatly curious. He replied,

"It is a long and rapid walk to some distant spot. To-day they have been to the top of Purple Mountain."

"Why?" I asked in great surprise.

"They consider this a pleasure," he answered.

It is very strange. Here even a farm woman would consider it a hardship to walk so far. When I said this to my brother he replied,

"Her life in her own country has been very free. She feels restrained in this little garden behind these high walls."

I was greatly surprised to hear this. It seems to me this life of ours can certainly be considered wholly modern and independent of old restraints. The garden wall is merely for privacy. It would not be fitting for any vegetable vendor or passing candy seller to peer at us. I thought,

"What will she do in the courtyards, then?"

But I said nothing.

❅

She is frank to show her love for my brother. Last night we sat in the garden to catch the coolness of the night. I sat in my accustomed place upon the porcelain seat, a little apart from the men. She seated herself beside me upon the low brick balustrade that surrounds the terrace, and in her half-smiling manner now when we are together, she pointed out one thing after another in the dim twilight, asking me the name of each and repeating the words after me. She is quick to learn, and she never forgets once she has heard rightly. She repeated each syllable over again and again softly, tasting its intonation, laughing a little when I corrected her shyly. Thus we amused ourselves for a space while the two men conversed.

But when the dusk of night fell, and we could no

longer distinguish trees and flowers and stones, she became silent and restless. She turned her eyes toward my brother. At last she rose abruptly and went over to him with her swinging gait, the thin white stuff of her gown flying like a mist. She laughed, said something in a low voice to him, and then stopped at his side and reached openly for his hand.

I averted my eyes.

When I glanced again, pretending to feel the direction of the wind, she had curled herself upon the brick floor of the terrace beside his chair and had laid her cheek against his hand! I felt a pang of sympathy for my brother. He must have been ashamed at this open display of passion from a woman. I could not see his face in the dark, but all talk had ceased. There was only the pulsing murmur of summer insects through the garden. I rose and withdrew myself.

When my husband came in a few minutes later I said to him,

"She is indecorous, this foreigner!"

But he only laughed.

[181]

"Oh, no—only to you, little porcelain one!"

Indignation pricked me.

"Would you have me then clinging to your hand in public?" I asked, turning to look at him.

He laughed again, his eyes on me.

"No, for if you did such a thing, how truly indecorous it would be!"

I perceived that he was laughing a little at me, and since I did not know why, I said nothing more.

I do not understand this freedom of hers. And yet, most strangely, when I ponder it I do not discern any evil insinuation in it. She avows her love for my brother as simply as a child may seek its playmate. There is nothing hidden or subtle in her. How strange this is! It is not like our women.

She is like the blossom of the wild orange tree, pure and pungent, but without fragrance.

They have agreed together at last what they will do. She is to put on Chinese dress, and together they will approach the honored Old Ones. My brother has taught her the proper way to bow in their presence. I am to go before to prepare the way and to take the gifts.

I cannot sleep at night for thinking of the hour. My lips are dry, and when I would moisten them, my tongue also is dry within my mouth. My husband endeavors to encourage me with laughter and bold words, but when he leaves me again, I am afraid. I am openly taking part against my mother, I who in all my life before have never disputed her will.

Where does the courage come from in me to do this thing? I am a timid creature always, and left to myself I would see nothing but evil in it. I see clearly even now my mother's heart in the matter. Alone, I would say that she is right according to the customs of our people.

It is my husband who has changed me, so that I dare, in spite of my fear, to speak for love even against my ancestors. But I tremble.

She, the foreigner, is the only calm one among us.

XV

To-day I am weary and spent, My Sister. In my heart it is as though a harp string had been too tightly drawn for many days and then suddenly relaxed, so that music is dead in it.

The hour I have dreaded is over! No, I will not say how it went. I will tell you of the whole matter, and then you may judge of it for yourself. As for me—but I will not tell of the end before the beginning.

We sent the messenger to our parents, bearing our request that we be allowed to present ourselves the next day at noon. He returned saying that our father had left home for Tientsin as soon as he heard of my brother's arrival. Thus did he avoid the difficult moment—thus has he ever avoided decisions! In his stead our mother appointed the hour of noon when she would receive my brother and me. Of the foreigner no mention was made, but my brother cried, "If I go, my wife will go, also."

I went first, therefore, the next day, at the hour, and a servant bore gifts before me. My brother had chosen these gifts in foreign countries, and they were all curious and pretty things not often seen in our city—a tiny gilt clock set in the stomach of a gilded child, the whole not more than six inches in height; a watch cunningly embroidered with jewels to wear upon the wrist; a machine which when wound with a handle could speak and shout; a light which renewed itself without fire, however long it shone; and a fan of ostrich plumes, white as a drift of pear blossoms.

I went into her presence with these gifts. Our mother had sent word that she would receive us in the guest-hall, and there she was seated, as I entered, in the heavy dark carved chair of blackwood, at the right of the table under the painting of the Ming Emperor. She was robed in black brocaded satin, and in her hair were ornaments of gold. Upon her hands were many rings of gold, set with rubies and topaz, the stones fitting for the dignity of age. She leaned upon her staff of ebony and silver. I had never beheld her more stately in outward appearance.

But I knew her well, and I scanned her face

closely to see how she really was in health, and my heart dropped in fear. The black of her garments but emphasized the transparent thinness of her face. So thin had she become that her lips had taken on the set curves almost of death itself, and her eyes had enlarged themselves, so that they were the sick and sunken eyes of the desperately ill. Upon her fingers the rings hung loosely and clattered against each other with a touch of dim music if she moved her hands. I longed to ask her how she really was, but I dared not, knowing it would annoy her. She had nerved herself to the meeting, and she had need of her strength.

Therefore when she received me without words, I presented the gifts, taking each from the hand of the servant and placing it before her. She acknowledged them with a grave inclination of the head, and without looking at them she motioned to her own servants who stood waiting near her, to remove them to another room. But her acceptance of them encouraged me somewhat. Had she declined them, in the language of gift-giving it would have meant that my brother was already refused. I said therefore,

"My honored mother, your son is here and awaits your pleasure."

"It has been told me," she replied coldly.

"He has brought the foreigner," I ventured faintly, thinking it best to tell the worst at once, and yet having at my heart a sinking of spirit.

She was silent. I could make nothing of her face. It was immovable.

"May they approach?" I asked desperately, not knowing what else to say than what we had planned.

"Let him approach," she replied in the same voice.

I hesitated, not knowing how to proceed. Was not the foreigner even then upon the very threshold? I went to the door where they stood waiting, and putting aside the curtain, I told my brother what our mother had said, and that he had better come first and alone.

His face darkened with the old look I remembered from his youth when something displeased him. He conversed a moment with that one in her own language. She lifted her eyebrows at his words and shrugged very lightly one shoulder, and stood

[187]

in calm and careless waiting. Then my brother seized her hand swiftly, and before I could stop them they had entered.

How strange a figure she was to enter the great hall of our ancestors! I stood clinging to the curtain, half-fascinated by the sight. The first of alien blood to cross this threshold! My wonder at the thought held my eyes to her, so that for a second I forgot my mother. Even while I knew half-consciously that my brother's determination not to enter alone must have stopped in an instant my mother's inclination toward him and her natural longing to see him again, I could not but marvel at the moment.

My brother had chosen clothing of our country for the foreigner to wear, a coat of dull blue silk, very heavy and soft and embroidered lightly with silver. Her skirt was of black satin, perfectly plain except as it hung in straightly planned folds, and on her feet he had caused to be placed black velvet shoes without embroidery. Above these dark colors her skin was white with the white luster of pearls under the moon, and her hair flared like yellow flames about her face. Her eyes were of the blue of stormy and thunderous skies, and her lips drooped in proud repose. She entered erect and haughty, her head thrown back. Her eyes met my mother's eyes without fear or smiling.

Seeing this, I pressed my hands to my mouth to repress a cry. Why had not my brother told her she should enter with downcast eyes before an elder? For his sake I regretted exceedingly her haughty bearing. She entered as the reigning queen might enter the presence of the imperial dowager.

My mother fixed her eyes upon the foreigner. Their eyes met, and instantly they declared themselves enemies. Then my mother turned her eyes haughtily away and gazed into space beyond the open door.

The foreigner said something to my brother in a calm voice. I knew afterwards it was this,

"Am I to kneel now?"

He nodded, and together they knelt before our mother, and my brother began to speak the words he had previously prepared,

"Most Ancient and Honorable, I am returned from foreign countries at your command, to the kind presence of my parents, I your unworthy son. I rejoice that our mother has seen fit to accept our useless gifts. I say 'our,' because I have brought with me my wife, of whom I wrote in a letter through the hand of my friend. She comes as the daughter-in-law of my mother. Although in her veins is foreign blood, she wishes me to tell our honorable mother that since she is married to me, her heart has become Chinese. She takes upon herself voluntarily the race and customs of our family. She renounces her own. Her sons will be altogether of our celestial nation, citizens of the Bright Republic, and heirs of the Middle Empire. She gives her homage."

He turned to the foreign one, who had been waiting quietly as he spoke, and gave her a signal. With surpassing dignity she bowed until her forehead touched the floor at my mother's feet. Three times did she bow, and then she and my brother bowed together three times more. Then they arose and awaited my mother's words.

For a long time she said nothing. Her eyes were still fixed, as they had been throughout, upon those open spaces of the courtyard beyond the door. Minutes she remained thus, silent, haughty, erect.

I think she was inwardly confused at my brother's

daring to disobey her by bringing the foreigner before her when she had said he was to come alone. I think she was silent, wondering how to meet the difficult moment. A spot of red came into either cheek, and in her delicate jaw I saw a muscle beat. But in her stately bearing there was no outward sign of confusion.

She sat with both hands folded upon the silver head of her cane. Her eyes did not waver as she gazed over their heads. The two waited before her. The silence in the hall became heavy with their waiting.

Then suddenly something broke the sternness of my mother's face. It changed. The color receded as quickly as it had come, and her cheeks became ashen. One hand fell loosely into her lap, and her eyes dropped uncertainly to the floor. Her shoulders drooped, and she shrank a little into her chair. She said with a hurried faintness,

"My son—my son—you are always welcome—to your home. Later I will talk—now you are dismissed."

My brother lifted his eyes then to her face and

searched it. He had not such a keen gaze as I, but even he knew something was wrong. He hesitated, then glanced at me. I saw that he wished to speak further, to remonstrate with her for her coldness. But I was alarmed for her. I shook my head at him. He spoke a word to the foreigner then, and they bowed and withdrew.

I flew to my mother's side then, but she motioned me away without a word. I longed to ask her forgiveness, but she would not allow me to speak. I could see that she was exhausted by some secret pain. I was not to be permitted to remain. I bowed therefore, and slowly I turned away. But from the court I looked back, and I saw her walking slowly back to her own apartments, leaning heavily upon two slaves.

Sighing, I returned to my home. I can make nothing of the future, ponder it as I may.

As for those two, my brother and the foreigner, those two who break my mother's heart, they went away for the rest of that day upon one of their long walks, and when night came they returned, and we did not speak together.

✳✳✳✳✳✳✳✳✳✳✳✳✳✳✳✳✳✳

XVI

You have been gone a long time, My Sister! Thirty
days? It is almost forty since I saw you—a full moon
and more! Was the journey peaceful? I thank the
gods that you are returned.

Yes, my son is well. He says everything now, and
the sound of his speech runs constantly through the
day like the running of a brook. He is silent only
on sleep. Such sweet speech, My Sister! His words
are soft and broken, and they move us to laughter,
only we cannot let him so much as see us smile, because if he knows we laugh at him, he is angered
and stamps his tiny feet. He considers himself altogether a man. You should see him stride beside his
father, stretching his fat legs to his father's quick
step!

You ask—? Ah, of her—of my brother's wife!
And my answer is a sigh. It is not well with my
brother. Yes, they are still here, still waiting. Nothing is decided. My brother is restless under this idle

passing of days which bring no decision. He has learned the impatience of the West, and he demands that his wishes come immediately to pass. He has forgotten that in our country time is nothing, and fates may remain unknown even when death has come. There is no haste which can hurry time here. —But I will tell you.

After they had presented themselves to my mother a circle of days passed, eight long days. We waited, but no word came. At first my brother expected hourly that some message must come. He would not allow the foreigner to unpack the great boxes they had brought, exclaiming,

"It is not worth while—it is only a day or two—"

He was unfixed in his behavior, laughing loudly and quickly at nothing, now gay, now suddenly silent, hearing nothing that was said to him. He was like one who listens without ceasing for some voice or sound which others in the room do not hear.

But when day lapsed into day and no message came for them, my brother grew angry and irritable and ceased his laughter at anything. He began to remember and review in his mind the hour of presentation to his mother, and he talked of it again and again, blaming now the foreign one for not being more humble before his mother, and blaming then his mother for her haughtiness, and declaring that his wife was right, and that it was foolish in these days of the republic to bow before anyone. Although when I heard this I could only marvel and say,

"Is our mother no longer our mother, then, since we have a republic?"

But he was impatient and vexed with everything and heard nothing that was said to him.

Although I must be just to the foreigner. She had not really objected to bowing before his mother. I am told she said only this,

"If it is your custom, of course I will do it, although I think it a little foolish, perhaps, to bow like that before anyone!"

She was calm, far calmer than my brother, and more confident of the future. She thought always of him and of how to win him back to happiness. Sometimes when she saw him angry she coaxed him away out into the garden or beyond the gate.

Once I looked at them out of the window, and I

saw them there in the garden. She was talking to him earnestly, and at last when he still did not answer her, but continued to look gloomily at the ground, she drew her hand gently along his cheek and gazed at him, half-smiling, half-wistful. I do not know what she said to him when they were alone like this, but afterwards my brother was better for a little while and more quiet, although he never eased his tension of waiting.

But she did not always coax him thus. Sometimes she shook her shoulders lightly in the way she had, and let him be alone. Only her eyes followed him with the deep look they have whenever she gazes at him. If he did not come to her then, she withdrew herself and spent the time in learning our language and in playing with my son, whom she loves and speaks to in words I cannot understand.

She has even begun to learn from me also something of the music of the ancient harp, and soon she knew enough to make an accompaniment to her songs. Her voice when she sings is full and moving in its depth, although to our ears, accustomed to the delicate, high notes of the human voice, it has a quality of sweet harshness. She can melt my brother to instant passion with her singing. I cannot understand the songs, but when I hear her I feel a dark vague pain.

At last when no message yet came from my mother, she seemed to cease to think of the matter and turned her mind to other things. She went daily for long walkings by herself or with my brother. I marveled that my brother ever allowed her to go alone, since it is certainly not seemly in a woman, but he said nothing, and she returned full of talk about the streets, wondering at sights which others would not notice and seeing beauty in strange places. I remember one day she came back smiling her quick smile, as though she had some inner amusement which others had not, and when my brother asked her concerning it she said, in her own language and he afterwards told it to us,

"I have seen the beauty of the earth when it has put forth grain. In the grain shop in the main street they have placed in little brown wicker baskets the loveliest colors of grains—yellow corn, red beans, dried gray peas, ivory sesame, pale honey-colored soy-beans, ruddy wheat, green beans—I never can pass them quickly. What a pastel I might make if I could dip a pencil into them!"

I could not understand what she meant altogether, but she is like that; she lives within herself, seeing beauty where others cannot. I had not thought of a grain-shop thus. It is true that the grains there are many-colored, but so it is by nature. No one has made the grains different. There is nothing to wonder at—it has always been thus. To us a grain-shop is only a place to buy food.

But she sees everything with strange eyes, although she seldom comments on anything, only asking questions and storing our answers away into her thoughts.

Living with her day after day, I have grown to like her, and as I watch her, there are times when I even see something of beauty in her strange looks and ways. Certainly she has a great pride of a kind. She is wholly frank and unconstrained in her bearing. Even to my brother, her husband, she is never humble. The strangest thing of all is that whereas in a Chinese woman he would not endure this, in her

[198]

he seems to find it a delight, bearing the sting of a pain, so that he is ever more enamored of her. When he sees her too long diverted by her study or her reading, or even by my son, he becomes restless and glances at her now and again and speaks to her, and at last if she does not heed him, he gives over his brooding and comes to her side, and she possesses him afresh. It is like nothing I have ever seen, this love between them.

But there came a day at last—I think it was the twenty-second after the presentation, when my mother sent for my brother, desiring him to come alone to her. The letter was kindly worded, even to gentleness, and we were all hopeful therefore, and my brother went immediately, and I waited with the foreigner for his return.

In an hour he was back! He strode into the front door and into the room where we sat. He was angry and his face was sullen, and he kept saying over and over that he would separate himself from his parents forever. At first we could get nothing ordered from his speech, but later, piecing this to that, we found something of the truth.

It seems he had gone before his mother full of tenderness and conciliation. But he said from the very first she was willing to concede nothing. She began by stressing her ill health.

"It is not long before the gods will remove me to another circle of existence," she said, and he was touched.

"Do not say that, my mother!" he begged of her. "You have a life yet to live in your grandchildren."

Instantly he regretted that he had given her the thought.

"Grandchildren?" she repeated quietly. "Ah, my son, from whence shall any grandchildren for me come, except from your loins? And the daughter of Li, my daughter-in-law, still waits, a virgin!"

Then without further polite speech she spoke plainly and urged him to marry his betrothed and give her a grandson before she died. He said then that he was already married. She said in anger to this that she would never accept the foreigner as his wife.

This much we have gathered together from what

he says. I do not know what more passed between them.

But Wang Da Ma, the faithful servant, says that she listened at the curtain, and that within a twist of the hand hot speech was flying back and forth, unseemly speech, between mother and son. It was like quick thunder crackling across the sky. She says my brother did indeed show patience until my mother threatened to have him disinherited from the family, and then he said bitterly,

"And will the gods give you another son, then, that you should throw this one away? Will they again enrich your womb at such an age? Or will you stoop to take the son of a concubine for your son?"

Unseemly words from a son, indeed!

Then he flung himself out of the doorway and rushed forth through the courtyards, cursing his own ancestors. There was a great silence within my mother's room, and then Wang Da Ma heard a moaning. It was my mother. Wang Da Ma entered in great haste. But my mother was instantly silent then and biting her lips merely bade the servant feebly to help her to her bed.

It is shameful that my brother should have spoken

thus to his mother! I do not excuse him for any cause. He should have remembered her age and her position. He thinks only of himself.

Oh, sometimes I hate the foreigner because she holds utterly in the palm of her hand my brother's heart! I longed to go at once to my mother, but my brother begged me to await her summons. My husband also commanded me to wait, since if I went it would seem to be against my brother, and now that he is eating our rice, this would be discourteous. I had therefore no recourse except in patience—poor food for an anxious heart, My Sister!

And thus matters remain with us.

Yesterday I was glad when Mrs. Liu came to see us. We had spent a difficult day, remembering the day before when my mother had been angered with my brother, so that their meeting bore no fruit except disappointment. My brother had hung about the rooms, scarcely speaking to anyone, and staring out of the window. If he picked up a book to read it, he threw it down quickly and chose another, only to put that away as quickly.

The foreigner, after observing him thus, with-drew into her own thoughts over a small book of her own. I busied myself with my son that I need not be about them. But so heavy was the disappoint-ment about the house that the cheerfulness of my husband coming in at noon for his rice scarcely lightened my brother's gloom, or broke the for-eigner's stillness. Therefore when in the afternoon Mrs. Liu came in, it was like a cool fresh wind blow-ing through the dull, sullen heat of a summer's day.

My brother's wife was seated with her book in her hand, held carelessly, as though she were half-dreaming over it. She stared a little at Mrs. Liu. We have had no visitors since my brother came; our friends have known of our difficult situation and have not come through delicacy, and we have in-vited no one, because we do not know how to in-troduce the foreigner. I call her my brother's wife in courtesy to him, and yet legally she is without position until my father and my mother recognize her.

But Mrs. Liu was wholly untroubled. She seized the foreigner's hand, and the two soon talked easily, and they even laughed. I do not know what they said, since they spoke in English. But the foreigner seemed suddenly awake, and I watched her, surprised at the change. She has these two selves, one silent, remote, even a little somber, and the other this gayety, which yet seems too intense for joy. Watching them I disliked Mrs. Liu for a little while because she seemed careless of the difficulty of our position. But when she rose to go she pressed my hand, and she said in our own language,

"I am sorry. It is hard for everyone."

She turned and said something to the other one, something which made her dark blue eyes suddenly silvery with tears. We stood and looked at each other then, the three of us, each hesitating on speech, when without warning the foreign one turned and went swiftly from the room. Mrs. Liu watched her, her face full of quiet pity.

"It is very hard for everyone," she repeated. "Is the affair between the two happy?"

Since she is frank like my husband, I answered without pretense,

"There is love between my brother and that one, but my mother is dying of her disappointment. You know how frail she is at best, now, as age comes on her."

She sighed and shook her head.

"I know—ah, yes, I see it often now. These are ruthless days for the old. There is no compromise possible between old and young. They are as clearly divided as though a new knife severed a branch from a tree."

"It is very wrong," I said in a low voice.

"Not wrong," she replied, "only inevitable. And that is the saddest thing in the world."

While we waited, therefore, helpless for a sign of what to do, I could not forget my mother. I pondered what Mrs. Liu had said, that these were sorrowful days for the aged, and to ease myself I said,

"I will take my son to visit his father's parents. They also are aged and longing."

My heart was softened to all those who are old. I dressed my son then in his long satin coat like his father's. On his first birthday we had bought him a hat like a man's, of black velvet, fitting his head closely, and with a red button on top. This I placed on his head. I touched his chin, his cheeks, and his forehead with a brush dipped in vermilion. When he was ready, he was so beautiful that I was frightened lest the gods consider that he was too lovely for a human being and be moved to destroy him.

And so his grandmother thought when she saw him. She lifted him against her, and her round cheeks shook with pleasure and laughter. She smelled his fragrant flesh, and she said again and again in a sort of ecstasy,

"Ah, my little one—ah, my son's son!"

I was moved by her emotion and reproached myself that I had not brought him more often to her. I could not regret that we had taken him for ourselves; this was part of that inevitable of which Mrs. Liu spoke. But I was sorry for anyone who must grow old without his continual presence. I stood smiling therefore as she adored the child. Then she looked at him afresh and said quickly, turning his face from side to side with her hands upon his cheeks,

"But what is this? You have done nothing to protect him from the gods! What carelessness is this?" Then turning to the slaves she cried, "Bring a gold earring and a needle!"

I had thought before this that I ought to pierce his left ear and place a gold ring in it to deceive the gods into thinking him a girl and useless to them. It is an ancient device against early death for an only son. But you know, My Sister, how tender is his flesh; my own flesh shrank in pain for him even now, although I dared not dispute my mother-in-law's wisdom.

But when she had placed the needle against the lobe of his tiny ear he cried out, and his eyes grew large with fear, and he drew his mouth down, so that his grandmother seeing it could not go on, and she dropped the needle. Then murmuring to him she called for a bit of red silk thread, and with that she tied the ring about his ear without piercing his flesh. Then he smiled, and his smile caught our hearts together.

Seeing what my son is to his grandmother I came away understanding yet more fully the pain of my mother. The fruit of her life is her grandson who is not yet born.

But I am happy that I made glad the heart of my son's grandmother, and I am eased a little of my grief for the aged.

※

The gods are pleased that I was filial and took the child yesterday to his father's mother, My Sister, for this morning a messenger came to us with a letter from my mother. It was addressed to my brother, and it said nothing of their angry words; it simply commanded my brother to come home. She said that she would take no further responsibility about the foreigner. The matter was too great for her. It must be decided by our father and by the male heads of the clan.

But meanwhile, she said, my brother could bring her home with him, and she could live in the outer court. It would not be fitting to have her mingle with the concubines and the children. Then the letter ended.

We were all astonished at the change in my mother's mind. My brother was at once altogether hopeful. He exclaimed over and over again with smiles,

"I knew she could give up her determination in the end! After all, I am her only son!"

When I reminded him that in no sense had she accepted the foreigner he replied,

"Once she is within the gates everyone will love her."

I said nothing then, since I did not wish to discourage him. But in my heart I knew that we Chinese women do not love others so easily. It is more likely that the women will remember the daughter of Li who waits for the consummation of her marriage.

I questioned secretly the messenger from my mother, and he replied that during the previous night my mother had been very ill so that they all feared that even at that moment she might pass over into the abode of the dead. But they caused prayers to be said and priests to be called, and she was better, and by the morning she had miraculously recovered sufficiently to write the letter with her own hand.

I understood at once what had happened. Seeing

death approach she feared that her son would never return to his home and his duty, and at that moment she vowed that she would summon him if the gods would spare her life.

My heart ached for her humiliation, and I longed to go to her at once, but my husband said,

"Wait! She has strength but for one thing at a time. For the weak, even sympathy is too heavy to be borne."

I restrained myself therefore, and helped my brother's wife to pack her boxes. If I could talk to her freely in our own language I would say,

"Remember that she is aged and suffering, and that you have taken away from her all that she had."

But I can say nothing because our speech together is broken with words not understood.

※

To-day my brother and his wife have removed themselves to his ancestral home. They will live in the old apartments where my brother spent his youth. She will not be allowed to sleep or eat or linger in the women's apartments. Thus my mother still refuses to recognize her.

[210]

Now that they are gone, I am glad to be alone with my husband and my child, and yet with their going some life has departed from the house. It is as if the west wind departed at sunset and left stillness that was yet a little dead.

I think of them and picture them in the old rooms alone together. I said to my husband last night,

"What will come of all this trouble?"

He shook his head in doubt. Then he said,

"With those two under one roof, the old and the young, it is iron meeting flint. Who can tell which will crush the other?"

"And what will come of it?"

"Fire of some sort will come of it," he replied gravely. "I pity your brother. There is no man able to stand unmoved between two proud women, one of them old and one of them young, and both loving him supremely."

He took our son upon his knee and regarded the child thoughtfully. I do not know what was in his mind. But the child innocently lifted the lock of hair over his ear in pride to display the ring his grandmother had hung there, crying,

"See, Da-da?"

Instantly we forgot my brother and his wife. My husband looked at me with suspicion and reproach.

"Kwei-lan, what is this?" he asked. "I thought we were done with this superstitious nonsense!"

"Your mother placed it there," I faltered, "and I had not the heart—"

"Nonsense!" he cried. "We must think of the child first! We cannot let him be given such ideas."

And taking out from his pocket a small knife, he carefully cut the silken thread that held the ring. Then leaning he threw it all out of the window into the garden below. When the child pouted, he said laughing,

"You are a man like me! See, I do not wear a ring in my ear like a woman. We are men. We are not afraid of gods!"

And the child smiled at his gay words.

But in the darkness of the night I thought of it half-afraid. Can age be forever wrong? What if after all there are gods? I would leave nothing undone for my son. Ah, how I understand my mother!

XVII

I DID not visit my mother's home for twenty days. I was weary and a little unwell, and when I thought of my mother and of my brother, the confusion of my mind increased. When I remembered my husband, my heart turned to my brother, and when I held my son in my arms, my heart cleaved to my mother.

Moreover, my mother did not send for me, and had I gone unbidden I should not have known how to greet her or to explain my coming. But staying much alone in the quiet house—you know how my son's father works all day and into the night—I wondered and imagined many things.

How was the foreigner spending the long, lingering days? Had my mother seen her again and spoken to her? I knew the slaves and the concubines would be excited and would watch her from behind corners, and the servants would make excuses to fetch tea for my brother and this thing and that in order to see her, and the talk in the kitchen quarters would be about her and her ways and her looks, her bearing and her speech, ending always in reproach that she was there at all and pity for the daughter of Li.

At last my brother came to see me. I sat one morning embroidering a pair of shoes for my son —you know it is only seven days more until the festival of Clear Spring—and suddenly the door opened and my brother came in unannounced. He wore Chinese dress, and he looked more as he did in his youth than at any time since his return. Only his face was grave. He sat down and began talking without greeting, as though we continued the conversation from some previous hour.

"Will you not come, Kwei-lan? My mother is very feeble, and I think she is ill. Her will alone remains as strong as ever. She has made a decree that for a year my wife must follow the life of a Chinese woman in the courts. Since my whole inheritance depends on her obedience, we are trying to follow my mother's wishes. But it is like caging a golden oriole! Come and bring the child."

He rose and walked restlessly about the room, and when I saw his distraction I promised him.

I went therefore that same afternoon to visit my mother, thinking that I might on the way through the courtyards stop to see that other one, my brother's wife. I dared not allow my mother to know that I came to see anyone else except her alone, and indeed I was determined that I would not even mention the foreigner to my mother unless she gave me opportunity.

I went straight into my mother's presence without lingering in the courts, although as soon as I came into the women's quarters the Second Lady came to the threshold of the moon-gate and beckoned to me from behind an oleander tree. But I merely bowed and passed on into my mother's presence.

After my greetings were over we spoke first of my son, and then I took courage to examine my mother's face. I thought her looking a little better, in spite of my brother's words, or at least not as ill as I had feared. I did not question her therefore of

her health, knowing that such inquiries always ir-
ritated her, although she never failed to answer
courteously. I asked instead,

"How do you find your son, my brother, changed
by his years away?"

She lifted her pointed eyebrows slightly.

"I have scarcely spoken to him of anything of importance. The question of his marriage to the daughter of Li of course awaits his father's coming. But
he seems more like himself, at least, since I sent word
that he was to wear his accustomed clothes when he
returned home. I was not pleased to see my son's
legs in trousers like a water-carrier's."

Since she had spoken of his marriage I affected
to ask carelessly, examining the pattern upon the
silk of my robe,

"And how do you find the blue-eyed foreigner?"

I was conscious of a stiffening in my mother's
body, but she merely coughed and then answered
with negligence in her voice,

"As for that one, the foreigner within the courts,
I know nothing about her. I sent for her once to
prepare my tea, since your brother tired me with his

beseeching that she be allowed to come into my presence. But I found I could not endure her awkward hands and barbarous looks. She was very clumsy about my person. I perceive that she has never been trained in the proper behavior to an elder. I shall not try to see her again. I am happier when I can forget the matter and remember only that my son is again under the ancestral roofs."

I was surprised that my brother had not told me that she had been called to make tea for our mother. It was a moment of importance. But when I considered I decided that he had purposely not told me of it, since she had been so unpleasing to our mother. But remembering my brother's anxiety I asked further, greatly daring,

"May I invite her to spend an hour in my poor house, since she is a stranger here?"

She answered coldly,

"No, you have done enough. I shall not allow her to go outside the great gate again so long as she remains here. She must learn the seclusion proper to ladies if she is to live here. I do not care to have the whole city talking of the matter. I perceive she is lawless and unrestrained, and she must be controlled. Speak no further of her."

The rest of our talk was carefully of nothing. I saw that she would not speak of anything below the surface of each day's casual happenings—the salting of the vegetables for the servants, the rise in the price of cloth for the children's clothes, the promise of the chrysanthemum slips now being planted for the autumn's flowering. I said farewell, therefore, and went away.

But as I passed outward through the small gates, I met my brother. He was going to the great gate-house, outwardly to ask some question of the gate-man, but I knew at once that he meant to wait there for me. When I drew near to him I scanned his face and saw that the vigor and determination which had made him foreign-looking in my eyes had given way to bewilderment and anxiety, which with his Chinese robes and his drooping head, made him look again like the schoolboy, half-sullen, that he had been before he went away.

"How is she, your wife?" I asked before he spoke.

His lips trembled; he passed his tongue over them.

"Not well. O my sister! We cannot long endure this life. I shall have to do something—go away and find work—"

He stopped, and I urged him then to have patience before he decided to break away. It was much that our mother allowed the foreigner to come into the court, and a year was not long. But he shook his head.

"My wife herself has begun to despair," he said heavily. "Until we came here she did not lose heart. But now she droops from day to day. Our food is distasteful to her—and I cannot procure foreign food for her. She eats nothing. In her own land she has been accustomed to freedom and homage. She is accounted beautiful, and many men have loved her. I was proud to win her from them all. I thought it proved the superiority of our race.

"But now she is like a flower plucked and placed in a silver vase, but without water. Day after day she sits silent, and her eyes burn in her white and whiter face."

I marveled to hear my brother hold it a virtue in

a woman to have been loved by many men. Here it would be considered praise for none but a harlot. How could she indeed ever hope to become one of us! But as he spoke a new thought had come into my mind.

"Does she desire to return to her own people?" I asked eagerly.

Here I saw a solution. If she would go away and the seas stretch again between them, my brother who is, after all, but a man, would cease to think of her, and he would return to his duty. But I shall not soon forget his look when I said this. His eyes seemed to fly at me with anger.

"If she goes, I will go with her," he said with sudden violence. "If she dies in this my home I am no more the son of my parents, forever!"

I chided him gently for such unfilial words, when, to my great astonishment, he burst into a harsh sob and turning, he walked quickly away.

I stood there, scarcely knowing what to do, watching his bowed figure recede into the other court where he lived, and then irresolutely, and indeed, half fearing my mother, I followed him.

I went in then to see the foreigner. She was walking restlessly about the inner court of my brother's apartment. She wore her foreign garb again, a straight robe of a dark blue color, cut away to leave bare her white throat. In her hand was a foreign book, open, and covered with short lines of letters running across the middle of each page in little groups.

She walked about reading and frowning as she read, but when she saw me, her face changed with her smile, and she stood still until I was at her side. We spoke a few words then, casual words. She could converse quite well now if one spoke of simple matters. I refused to go in, saying I must return to the child, and she was sorry. I mentioned the ancient juniper in the court; she spoke of a toy she was making for my son from cloth stuffed with cotton. I thanked her—and there was no talk left. I waited, then I began my farewell, aching with vague pain, because the seas are between us, and I could do nothing to help my brother or my mother.

But when I turned to leave she suddenly seized my hand and held it fast. I looked at her then, and I saw her shake tears from her eyes with a quick fling of her head. Pity filled me, and I murmured to her, not knowing what to say except to promise to come again soon. Her lips trembled while she tried to smile.

Thus passed yet another moon. Then my father returned home. Strangely enough, he took a great interest in my brother's wife and found a liking for her. Wang Da Ma said that as soon as he entered the great gate he inquired whether or not my brother had brought the foreigner home, and when he heard it, he changed his robes and sent word that he would visit my brother's apartments as soon as he had eaten.

He entered, suave and smiling, and accepted the obeisances of my brother and demanded to see the foreigner. When she came in he laughed a great deal and examined her appearance and commented freely upon her looks.

"She is handsome enough in her way," he announced in great good nature. "Well, well, it is a new thing in the family. And can she speak our language?"

My brother was displeased with his freedom and replied briefly that she was learning. My father laughed immoderately and cried,

"Never mind—never mind—I suppose love-words sound as sweetly in a foreign tongue—heh-heh-heh!" And he laughed until his fat body shook.

As for her, she could not understand all his words, spoken carelessly, as he always speaks, in his rich, thick voice, but his friendliness cheered her; and my brother could not well tell her that his father was lacking in respect to her.

I am told that my father visits her often now and toys with her, gazing at her freely and teaching her new words and expressions. He has sent her sweetmeats and once a Buddha's hand lemon tree in a green glazed pot. My brother, however, takes care to be present at all these meetings.

She is like a child. She understands nothing at all.

I went to see my brother's wife again yesterday, after I had given my mother greeting for the feast day. I do not dare to risk my mother's displeasure

by more than passing visits to the foreigner, lest I be forbidden altogether to go into my brother's courts.

"You are happier?" I asked her.

She smiled her quick smile. It always lightens her grave face like sudden sun from behind a somber cloud.

"Yes, perhaps!" she answered. "At least things are no worse with us. I have not seen his mother except once when she wanted me to make tea. I had never made tea in my life like that before! But his father comes to see us nearly every day."

"We will have patience," I replied. "The day will yet come when the August Mother will relent."

Instantly her face hardened.

"It is not as though I had done anything," she said in a low compressed voice. "Surely it is not a fault to love and to marry? His father is the only friend I have in this house. He is kind to me, and I need kindness I can tell you! I do not think I can stand it much longer, locked up like this!"

She shook back her short yellow hair, and then suddenly her eyes grew dark and angry. I saw she

[224]

was looking out into the other courts, and my eyes followed hers.

"Look at that, again!" she cried. "There they are —I am like a play for those women! I am weary to death of their staring. Why are they always there whispering and peeping and pointing?"

She nodded as she spoke at the moon-gate. There, gathered about its entrance, were the concubines and half a dozen slaves. They were idly eating peanuts and feeding them to their children, but secretly they were peering at the foreigner and I could hear them laughing. I frowned at them but they pretended not to see me, and at last she drew me further into the room with her and slid fast the heavy wooden doors against them.

"I cannot bear them," she said passionately. "I cannot understand what they say, but I know they talk about me from morning until night."

I soothed her,

"You must not mind them. They are altogether ignorant."

But she shook her head, saying,

"I cannot keep bearing it day after day."

She frowned and was silent and seemed to be thinking, and I waited, and we sat there together in the big dim room. I looked about me at last, since there was nothing more to be said, and observed the changes she had made, to make the room, I suppose, more western in its appearance. But to my eyes it only looked very odd.

A few pictures hung without order upon the walls, and among them were some photographs framed. When she saw me looking at them her face cleared, and she said eagerly,

"Those are my parents and my sister."

"You have no brother?" I asked.

She shook her head, and her lips curled a little.

"No, but it does not matter. We do not care only for our sons."

I wondered a little at her tone, but I did not understand it, and I rose to examine the pictures. The first was a picture of a grave old man with a short white pointed beard. His eyes were like hers, stormy and heavy-lidded. His nose was high, and he had a bald head.

'He taught—he is a professor in the college where

we first met, your brother and I," she said, her eyes
fixed fondly on the old man's face. "It is strange to
see him here in this room. He does not fit here—any
more than I seem to," she added in a low rueful
voice. "But it is my mother's face that I cannot bear
to look at these days!"

She had come up and was standing beside me
very tall above me, but now she turned away from
the second picture and went back to the chair from
which she had risen, and picked up some white cloth
that lay on the table near, and began to sew. I had
never seen her sew before. She placed on her finger
a curious metal cap, not at all like a real thimble
that circles one middle finger, and she held the
needle like a dagger. But I said nothing. I went to
observe the face of the mother. It was very small
and delicate and kind in its own way, although its
decorum was marred by the manner in which the
white hair was massed about it. The face of the
sister was distinctly like it, although very young
and laughing. I said politely,

"You long very much to see your mother?"

But to my surprise she shook her head.

"No," she said in her abrupt fashion. "I cannot even write to her."

"Why?" I asked in surprise.

"Because I am afraid that all she feared for me is coming true. I would not for anything have her see me as I am here! And she knows me well enough to see me clearly if I write. I have not written once since I came to this place.

"Oh, there in my home it all seemed wonderful —my little sister thought it was the most perfect romance imaginable and I—you do not know how perfect a lover he can be. He used to say things in such a way that every other man's love-making was wearisome and stale. He made love seem new. But my mother was always afraid—always!"

"Afraid of what?" I asked, wondering.

"That I would not be happy coming so far—that his people would not—that they would do something to make it all come wrong. And I feel it is all beginning to go wrong, perhaps! I do not know—but a net seems gathering in around me. Locked in behind these high walls I imagine things—I cannot

understand what they say—these people—I do not
know what they mean. Their faces never tell anything. I get afraid in the night.

"And then sometimes I even think I see his face
like theirs, smooth and covered and revealing nothing of what he feels. Over there in my own home,
he seemed like one of us, only more charming with
a new charm I had never seen before. But here he
seems to slip back into strangeness—slip away from
me. Oh, I do not know how to express it! I have
always been used to frankness and cheerfulness and
speaking straight out. And here it is all silence and
bowing and sliding eyes at me. I could bear being
cut off from my freedom like this if I knew what
was behind it all. But—do you know, I told him over
there at home that I could be a Chinese or a Hotten-
tot or anything for him—but I cannot, I cannot! I
am forever American!"

All this she poured forth, half in her own language, half in the little she knows of ours, her eyebrows twisting, her hands moving, her whole face
disturbed. I never dreamed so much speech was in

her. She poured it forth as water gushes suddenly from a sealed rock. I was highly embarrassed by it, since I had never seen a woman's heart so naked, and yet some sort of vague pity stirred in me in answer to her.

But while I was thinking what to say to her, and as though he had heard it all, my brother came in from his room next to us, and ignoring me he went to her and took the hands she had dropped upon her work. He knelt beside her and pressed her hands, still clasped, against his cheek, and then placed them over his eyes and put his head down. I hesitated, not knowing whether to go or stay. Then he looked up at her with a haggard face. He whispered in a hoarse voice,

"Mary, Mary, I never heard you talk like that! You do not really doubt me? In your country you told me you would take my race and nationality upon you and share it. Well, if it is impossible at the end of this year, we will leave it all behind us, and I will become American with you. And if that is impossible, then we will found a new country and a new race somewhere—so that we can be together. You must not doubt me, indeed, O my love!"

This much I understood of what he said, for he spoke in his own tongue for greater freedom. Then he began murmuring to her in another language, and I do not know what it was he told her. But she smiled, and I saw that she could endure yet much more for his sake. She dropped her head until it rested on his shoulder, and they fell into a throbbing silence, and I was ashamed to remain longer in the uncovered presence of this love.

I slipped quietly out therefore and found relief in scolding the slaves for staring through the gate at her. I could not of course reproach my father's concubines, but I took care to speak to the slaves in their hearing. But none had anything in them but ignorant and even impudent curiosity. The fat concubine said, chewing loudly and smacking her lips over an oily cake,

"Anyone so ridiculous and inhuman in appearance must expect to be looked at—and laughed at as well!"

"Nevertheless, she is human, and she has feelings like ours," I answered as sternly as I could.

But the Second Lady only shrugged her thick shoulders and chewed on, wiping her fingers carefully upon her sleeve.

I came away angry and was nearly at my own home before I realized that my anger was wholly for my brother's wife, and no longer against her!

✲✲✲✲✲✲✲✲✲✲✲✲✲✲✲✲✲✲

XVIII

AND now, My Sister, what we have not desired has
come to pass—she has conceived! She was already
aware of it for a whole circle of days, before, with
curious foreign reserve, she even told my brother,
who has just told me.

It is not a thing to make us rejoice, and my
mother, hearing of it, has taken to her bed, and she
cannot rise for sorrow. It is what she has feared and
dreaded, and her fragile body cannot stand against
the strength of her disappointment. You know how
she has desired the first-fruits of my brother's flesh
for the family. And now since that can never be,
she thinks that virtue has gone out of him for nothing, since this child can never stand before her as a
grandson.

I went to my mother then, and I found her lying
straight and still upon her bed. Her eyes were closed,
and she opened them only enough to recognize me
before she closed them again. I sat down quietly

beside her and waited in silence. Suddenly her face changed, as it had that other day; it deadened to the dreadful hue of ashes, and she began to breathe heavily.

I was frightened, and I clapped my hands for a slave, and Wang Da Ma herself came running with an opium pipe lit and smoking. My mother grasped it and sucked at it desperately, and the pain was relieved.

But when I saw this my spirit was ill at ease. Evidently the pain was habitual, since the opium pipe was kept prepared and the lamp burning. When I sought to speak of it, however, my mother forbade me, saying sharply,

"It is nothing. Do not annoy me."

She would say nothing more than that, and after remaining a little while beside her, I bowed and came away. When I passed through the servants' court I asked Wang Da Ma concerning my mother, and she shook her head.

"The First Lady suffers this way each day more times in number than the fingers on both my hands. The pain has been occasional for many years, yet you know she will never speak of her own affairs.

But under the sorrows of this year the pain has become constant. I am always about her person, and I see the grayness pass over her face. I see her face broken with pain at early dawn when I take in the tea. But some hope has sustained her of late until the last few days. Now she has dropped like a tree whose last root has been chopped away."

She took up the corner of her blue apron and wiped each eye in turn and sighed.

Ah, I know the hope which has sustained my mother! I said nothing, but I returned to my home, and I wept, and I told my husband. I begged him to go with me to see her, but he counsels me to wait. He says,

"If she is forced or angered, she will be worse. When the opportune time comes, implore her to see a physician. Further than this you have no responsibility with an elder."

I know he is always right. But I cannot cast aside my sense of portending evil.

It seems my father is pleased that the foreign one is to bear a child. He cried when he heard of it,

"Ah ha! Now we will have a little foreigner to play with! Hai-ya! A new toy, indeed! We will call him Little Clown, and he shall amuse us!"

My brother muttered at these words. He begins to hate our father in his heart. I can see it.

As for the foreign one, she has given up her mournfulness. When I went to see her to congratulate her she was singing a weird, harsh, foreign tune. When I inquired its meaning, she said it was a song of sleep for a child. I marvel that any child could rest, hearing it. She seems to have forgotten that she ever uncovered her unhappiness to me that day. She and my brother have renewed their love, and she has room for nothing else in her mind, now that the child is coming.

In my heart I am anxious to see this foreign child. He cannot be beautiful as my son is beautiful. It may even be a girl, and perhaps she will have the fire-yellow hair of her mother. Ah, my poor brother!

He is unhappy, my brother! Now that a child is to be born, he is more than ever anxious to establish his wife's legal position. He hints of the matter daily to our father, but our father puts him off with smiling, leisurely talk of other things.

At the next feast day my brother says he will press the matter before the clan, even in the ancestral hall before the sacred tablets of the ancestors, so that the child may be born legally as his eldest son. Of course if it is a girl, it will not matter. But we can discern nothing of the future.

It is now the eleventh moon of the year. Snow lies upon the ground, and the bamboos are heavy with it in the garden, so that they are a frothing sea of white waves when the wind stirs them gently. My brother's wife grows great with child. At my mother's house there is a heavy sense of waiting. For what? I ask myself daily.

This day when I rose from my bed I saw the trees bare and blackened against a gray and wintry sky. I waked suddenly and in fear, as from an evil dream; yet when I examined my memory, I had dreamed of nothing. What is the meaning of our life? It is in the hands of the gods, and we know nothing except fear.

I have tried to discover why I am afraid. Is it for my son? But he is a young lion for strength. He talks now like a king, commanding the world. Only his father dares to disobey him with laughter. As for me, I am his slave, and he knows it. He knows everything, the rogue! No, it is not my son.

But however I reason of the matter, I cannot cast aside my restlessness, my instinct of future evil about to descend on us from heaven. I am waiting for the gods to make it known. I am certain of their malevolent purpose. Can it be after all for my son? I am half-fearful still about the casting away of the ring.

His father laughs. It is true that the child is sound from head to foot. His appetite is enough to astonish me. He thrusts aside my breast now, and he demands rice and chopsticks thrice daily. I have weaned him, and he is a man. Ah, no, it is never anyone so strong as my son!

My mother grows more feeble. I wish that my father had not gone away. When my brother became importunate concerning his wife, my father found business in Tientsin, and he has been absent for many moons. But now when evil hangs over his house he should return. Careful as he ever has been of his own pleasure only, still he should remember that he is the representative of his family before Heaven.

Yet I dare not write him, I, a mere woman and ridden by a woman's fears. It may all be nothing. But if it is nothing, then why does day follow day, in this rigid expectancy?

I have taken incense and burned it before Kwanyin secretly, dreading my husband's laughter. It is all very well not to believe in the gods when there is no trouble approaching. But when sorrow hangs over a house, to whom shall we appeal? I prayed to her before my son was born and she heard me.

This day ushers in the twelfth moon. My mother lies motionless upon her bed and I begin to fear that she will never rise from it. I have besought her to call physicians, and at last she was willing, being,

I fear, weary of me. She has invited Chang, that famous doctor and astrologer, to attend her. She has paid him forty ounces of silver, and he promises her recovery. I have been comforted since he says this, for everyone knows he is wise.

But I wonder when the hour of relief will begin. She smokes the opium pipe incessantly now, to dull the pain in her vitals, and she is too drowsy for speech. Her face is dull yellow, and the skin is stretched over the bones until it is dry and paper thin to the touch.

I have begged her to see my husband that he may try the western medicines, but she will not. She mutters that she has been young and now she is old, but she will never endure the ways of the barbarians. As for my husband, he shakes his head when I speak to him of my mother. I can see that he thinks she is about to enter upon the Terrace of Night.

O my mother—my mother!

❋

My brother says nothing from morning until night. He broods. He sits in his own apartment, staring and frowning, and when he moves out of himself it is only to express a frenzy of tenderness towards his wife. They have gone together into an existence of their own, a world where they dwell alone with their unborn child.

He has caused a screen to be woven of bamboos and placed over the moon-gate so that the idle women can no longer peer in at her.

When I speak to him of our mother he is deaf. He says over and over like an angry child,

"I can never forgive her—I can never forgive her!"

Never in his life before has he been refused anything, and now he cannot forgive his mother!

For many weeks, one after the other, he did not go to see her. But yesterday he was moved a little at last by my fears and my beseechings, and he went with me and stood beside her bed. He stood in stubborn silence, refusing to greet her. He looked at her, and she opened her eyes and looked at him steadily without a word.

Nevertheless when we withdrew from her presence together, although he would not speak then of her even to me, yet I could see that he was shaken by her sick face. He had suspected that some bitter determination against him kept her in her own room, but now he saw that she was mortally ill. Therefore, once each day after that, Wang Da Ma said, he took a bowl of tea in his two hands and presented it himself to his mother, without words.

Sometimes she thanked him faintly, but beyond that they have had no speech together since it has been made known that his wife is with child.

My brother has sent a letter to our father, and to-morrow he comes.

My mother has not spoken now for many days. She lies in a heavy sleep which is yet not like any sleep we have ever seen. Chang the doctor has shrugged his shoulders and spread out his hands and said,

"If Heaven ordains death, who am I to stay that supreme destiny?"

He has taken his silver and thrust his hands into his sleeves and departed. When he had gone I flew to my husband and besought him to come to my

mother. Now that she sees nothing that passes before her, she would not know whether he were
there or not. At first he would not, but when he saw
how I feared for her he came unwillingly and stood
beside her bed, and for the first time he saw my
mother.

I never saw him so moved. He looked at her for
a long time, and then he shuddered from head to
foot and came quickly away. I wondered if he were
ill but when I questioned him he only said,

"It is too late—it is too late."

And then he turned to me suddenly, crying,

"She looks so much like you that I thought of
your face lying there dead!"

And we wept.

I go daily to the temple now where I have been
scarcely at all since my son was born. Having him I
have had nothing more to desire of the gods. They
have become angry at my happiness, therefore, and
have punished me through her, my beloved mother.
I go to the god of long life. I have placed sacrifices

before him of flesh and of wine. I have promised a hundred rounds of silver to the temple if my mother recovers.

But I have no response from the god. He sits immovably behind his curtain. I do not even know whether or not he receives my sacrifices.

Underneath all our lives, behind the veil, these gods are plotting!

❋

O My Sister, My Sister! The gods have spoken at last and have showed us their wickedness! *Look!* I am robed in sackcloth! See my son—he is wrapped from head to foot in the coarse white cloth of mourning! It is for her—for my mother! O my mother, my mother! Nay—do not stay my weeping —I must weep now—for she is dead!

I sat alone with her at midnight. She lay as she has lain these ten days, a thing of bronze—immovable. She had not spoken or eaten. Her spirit had already heard the call of the higher voices, and only her strong heart was left to beat itself out into feebleness and silence.

[244]

When the hour before dawn appeared, I saw with sudden fear that there was a change in her. I struck my hands together and sent the waiting slave for my brother. He sat in the outer room prepared for my summons. When he came in he looked at her and whispered half-afraid,

"The last change has come. Let someone go for our father."

He motioned to Wang Da Ma who stood by the bed wiping her eyes, and she withdrew to do his bidding. We stood hand in hand waiting, weeping and in awe.

Suddenly our mother seemed to rouse herself. She turned her head and gazed at us. She lifted her arms up slowly as though they bore a heavy burden, and she sighed deeply twice. Then her arms fell, and her spirit passed over, silent in passing as in life, revealing nothing.

When our father came in, half-asleep still, with his garments thrown hastily about his body, we told him. He stood before her staring and afraid. In his heart he has always feared her. Now he began to weep easy tears, like a child, and to cry loudly,

"A good wife—a good wife!"

My brother led him gently away then, soothing him and bidding Wang Da Ma to bring wine to comfort him.

Then I, left alone with my mother, looked again on the silent, stiffening face. I was the only one who had ever seen her truly, and my heart melted itself into hot and burning tears. I drew the curtains slowly at last and shut her away, back again into the loneliness in which she had lived.

My mother—my mother!

We have perfumed her body with the oil of acanthus flowers. We have wrapped her in length upon length of yellow silken gauze. We have placed her in one of the two great coffins made each of the trunks of immense camphor trees and prepared for her and for my father many years ago when my grandparents died. Upon her closed eyes lie the sacred jade stones.

Now the great coffin has been sealed. We have called the geomancer and consulted him to find the day ordained for her funeral. He has searched the book of the stars and has discovered that it is the sixth day of the sixth moon of the new year.

We have called priests, therefore, and they have come decked in the scarlet and yellow robes of their office. With the sad music of pipes and in solemn procession we have conducted her to the temple to await the day of burial.

There she lies under the eyes of the gods, in the stillness and the dust of the centuries. There is not a sound to break her long sleep; there is forever only the muffled chant of the priests at dawn and at twilight, and through the night the single note of the temple bell struck at long intervals.

I can think of no one but of her.

✹✹✹✹✹✹✹✹✹✹✹✹✹✹✹✹✹✹

XIX

CAN it be four moons have passed between us, My Sister? I wear in my hair the white cord of mourning for her, my Ancient One. Although I go about my life, I am not the same. The gods have cut me off from my source, from the flesh which formed my flesh, and the bone of which my bones are made. Forever I bleed at the point of separation.

Yet I ponder the matter. Since Heaven would not grant my mother her great desire, was it in kindness after all that the gods, seeing it, removed her whom they loved from a world of change she could never have understood? It is an age too difficult for her. How could she have endured what has come to pass? I will tell you everything, My Sister.

Scarcely had the funeral procession passed from the great gate before the concubines began to quarrel among themselves as to who should now be first. Each desired to be the First Lady in my mother's place, and each desired to wear the coveted red garments, which as Small Wives they had never been allowed. Each desired the privilege of being carried through the great gate at death, for you know, My Sister, a concubine in her coffin may pass only through a side gate. Each of the foolish ones bedecked themselves afresh to win again my father's glances.

Each, I say? I forget that one, La-may.

All these months, lingering now into years, she has been on the family estates in the country, and we forgot in the stress of the hour of my mother's death to write her; and it was ten days before the word was carried to her by the hand of my father's steward. Yes, she has lived there quite alone, save for the servants and her son, ever since there was talk of my father's adding a concubine after her. It is true that he never did it, since his interest in the woman waned before the matter was finally arranged, and he decided that she was not worth the amount of money demanded for her by her family. But La-may could not forget that he had desired another. She never came back to him, and since he hates the country, she has known that he would not come to her there.

But when she heard of my mother she came at once and went to the temple where my mother's body lay, and casting herself upon the coffin she wept silently for three days without food. When Wang Da Ma told me of it I went to her and raised her up in my arms and brought her to my own house.

She is changed indeed. All her laughter and restlessness is gone, and she dresses no longer in gay silks. She has ceased to paint her lips, and they are carven and pale in her pale face. She is still and gray and silent. Only the old scornfulness remains, and when she heard of the concubines' disputes among themselves her lips curled. She alone cares nothing to be first.

She avoids all mention of my father. I have heard that she has promised to take poison if he ever comes near her again. Thus has love curdled within her to hatred.

When she heard of the foreign wife of my brother she was silent as if she had heard nothing of what I said. When I spoke to her again of the matter, she

listened coldly and replied in a small voice as thin
and as sharp as ice,

"It is a great agitation and talk about something
which is already decided by nature. Can the son of
such a father be faithful? He is all passion now.
I know what that is. But wait until her child is
born, and her beauty is torn from her as a cover is
torn from a book. Does she think he will care to
read the book then, even though its pages speak of
nothing but love for him?"

And she was not interested. No other word did
she speak of my father during the four days she
was in my house. All that was once gayety and desire
for love in her has died. She is only angry now, always angry at everything, but her anger has no heat.
It is cold and reasonless, like a serpent's anger, and
full of venom. I was frightened of her sometimes,
and I told my husband after she had gone, and I put
my hand into his. He held my hand for a long time
between both of his, and at last he said,

"She is a woman scorned. Our old customs have
held women lightly, and she was not one who could
love easily and so endure it."

How terrible a thing is love unless it can flow fresh and unchecked from heart to heart!

As for La-may, she returned to the country after the period of mourning for my mother.

※

In the matter of the other concubines nothing could be decided until my brother's wife had been recognized, since his legal wife would be the natural one to take his mother's place as First Lady. The affair now became the more pressing because the house of Li, to whose daughter my brother was still betrothed, began to send messages almost daily through the go-between, urging that the marriage be consummated at once.

Of course my brother did not tell this to the foreign one, but I knew it, and I understood therefore why his face became harried and more anxious as these complications closed in around him. My father received the go-between and while my brother did not actually see them or hear their words, my father did not fail to repeat with affected carelessness and laughter what they said.

Since our mother's death my brother and the foreigner had renewed their love to each other, and this in itself made like a knife twisted in his vitals all talk to my brother of any other marriage. Although the foreigner had never loved my mother, nevertheless when my brother reproached himself at last for his harshness to his mother in her feebleness, and struck his breast when he thought of how he had hastened her end, she, his wife, bore with him most tenderly.

She listened to his remorse and turned his thoughts gently to the coming child and to the future. She is wise. A woman with a smaller mind would have resented his lamentations for his mother. But when he spoke of the virtues of his mother, as one will speak of those dead, she agreed with him, and with much grace she was silent concerning my mother's attitude toward herself. She even added to his praises her respect for the strength of my mother's spirit, turned against her as it was. Pouring himself out thus to his wife, my brother emptied his sorrow, and into that emptiness his love for his wife entered and filled him anew.

Together, then, they remained in their own courts, apart from everything. For a space I myself scarcely saw them. It was as though they lived alone in some far country, and nothing, no one, could touch them. When I went into their presence, although they always welcomed me, quickly and without knowing it they forgot me. Their eyes met secretly and spoke to each other, even while their lips spoke to me. If they were apart so much as the length of the room, they drifted nearer, unconscious of it themselves, but restless until they were within reach of each other.

I think it was during these days of renewal of love that my brother began to see clearly what he must do. A certain calm spread over his spirit as he became willing to give up everything for her, and his body ceased its restlessness.

Watching them I marveled that only warmth came into my heart for them. Had I ever seen them thus before my marriage I should have sickened at such emotion between man and wife. It would have been a sight without dignity in my eyes, since I could not have understood it. I should have belittled love itself and thought it fit only for concubines and slave-girls.

And now, you see how I am changed, and how my lord has taught me! I knew nothing indeed until he came.

Thus they lived together, waiting for the future, these two, my brother and his foreign wife.

And yet my brother was not wholly happy. *She* was happy! It was nothing to her now that she was not a member of my brother's family. With the passing of his mother, in spite of her sympathy, a sort of bondage dropped from her. With the knowledge of her child living within her, she was relieved of some fear she had had before. She thought of nothing now except her husband and herself and their child. Feeling the child stirring she smiled and said,

"It is this little person who will teach me everything. I will learn from him how to belong to my husband's country and race. He will show me what his father is like—what he was from the time he was a baby until manhood. I can never be separate and alone any more."

And again she said to her husband,

"It does not matter whether your family will receive me or not, now. Your bone and blood and brain have entered into my being, and I will give birth to the son of you and of your people."

But my brother was not satisfied with this law of the spirit. He reverenced her when she spoke thus, but he went from her presence, his anger hot against his father. He said to me,

"We can live alone forever, we two, but shall we deprive the child of his heritage? Have we the right if we would?"

But I could not answer him anything, for I do not know what is wise.

❃

When the time for the child's birth drew near, therefore, so that it might be hourly expected, my brother went yet once more to my father to ask his formal recognition of his wife. I will tell you, My Sister, what my brother told me.

He said he went into his father's apartments, trying to reassure himself with the favor which his father in the past had shown to his wife. While much that had been done and said was not courteous in meaning, yet my brother hoped that there might be some growth of real liking come out of it. He bowed his head before his father. He said,

"My honored Father, now that the First Lady, my honored mother, has departed to dwell beside the Yellow Springs, I, your unworthy son, beg you to deign to hear me."

His father was sitting beside the table drinking. Now he inclined his head, smiled, and still smiling, he poured wine from the silver jug and sipped it delicately from the tiny jade wine bowl in his hand. He answered nothing. My brother therefore was encouraged to continue.

"The poor flower from a foreign land now seeks to ascertain her position among us. According to western marriage customs we were legally married, and in the eyes of her countrymen she is my First Lady. She wishes to be established now according to the laws of our country. This is the more important since she is about to bear my first child.

"The Ancient First Lady has departed, and we mourn her loss forever. But it is necessary to place the First Lady of her son in the rightful order of generation. The foreign flower wishes to become one of us, to belong to our root, as a plum tree is grafted upon the parent stem, before it bears fruit. She wishes her children to belong to our ancient and celestial race forever. It remains now but for our father to recognize her. She is the further encouraged by our father's gracious favors to her in the past."

Still his father said nothing. He continued to smile. He poured forth more wine, and he drank again from the jade cup. At last he said,

"The foreign flower is beautiful. How beautiful are her eyes like purple jewels! How white, like almond meats, is her flesh! She has amused us well, has she not? I congratulate you that she is about to present you with a little toy!"

He poured wine from the jug and drank again, and continued with his usual affable manner.

"Sit down, my son. You fatigue yourself unduly."

He opened the drawer of the table and brought forth a second wine bowl and motioned my brother to seat himself. He poured the second bowl full of wine. But my brother refused it and continued to stand before him. His father went on speaking, his thick, soft voice rolling easily along,

"Ah, you do not love wine?" He smiled and sipped, and then wiping his lips with his hand, he smiled again. He said at last, seeing that my brother was determined to stand before him until he was answered,

"As for your request, my son, I will consider it. I am very busy. Moreover, your mother's passing has filled me with such sorrow that I cannot fix my mind now on any matter. To-night I go to Shanghai to find some diversion for my mind, lest I fall ill through excess of sorrow. Convey my compliments to the expectant one. May she bear a son like a lotus! Farewell, my son— Good son! Worthy son!"

He rose, still smiling, and passed into the other room and drew the curtain.

When my brother told me of all this, his hatred was such that he spoke of my father as of a stranger. Ah, we learned in the Sacred Edicts when we were only little children even, that a man must not love his wife more than his parents. It is a sin before the ancestral tablets and the gods. But what weak human heart can stem the flowing of love into it? Love rushes in, whether the heart will have it or not. How is it that the ancients in all their wisdom never knew this? I cannot reproach my brother any more.

Strangely enough, it is now the foreign one who suffers most keenly. The antagonism of my mother did not grieve her like this. She is broken-hearted over the carelessness of my father. At first she was angry and spoke coldly of him. She said when she heard what had passed between her husband and his father,

"Was all his friendliness pretense, then? I thought he really liked me. I felt I had a friend in him. What did he mean—oh, what a beast he is, really!"

I was shocked at such open speech concerning an elder and looked at my brother to see what he would say to reprove her. But he stood silent with bowed head, so that I could not see his face. She looked at him, her eyes wide as though in terror, and suddenly without warning, for her manner of speaking had been most cold and detached, she burst into sobbing and ran to him crying,

"Oh, dearest, let us leave this horrible place!"

I was amazed at her sudden emotion. But my brother received her into his arms and murmured to her. I withdrew myself, therefore, filled with pain for them and with doubt of the future.

✳✳✳✳✳✳✳✳✳✳✳✳✳✳✳✳✳

XX

Now has our father decided, My Sister! It is hard to receive his decision, but it is better to know it than to remain in false hope.

Yesterday he sent a messenger to my brother, a third cousin-brother, an official in the clan of my father's house. He bore our father's will to my brother in these words, when he had taken tea and refreshment in the guest hall.

"Hear, son of Yang. Your father replies plainly to your petition thus, and the members of the clan agree with him; even to the lowest they uphold him. Your father says,

"'It is not possible that the foreign one be received among us. In her veins flows blood unalterably alien. In her heart are alien loyalties. The children of her womb cannot be sons of Han. Where blood is mixed and impure the heart cannot be stable.

" 'Her son, moreover, cannot be received in the ancestral hall. How could a foreigner kneel before the long and sacred line of the Ancient Great? One only may kneel there whose heritage is pure, and in whose flesh is the blood of the Ancients unadulterated.'

"Your father is generous. He sends you a thousand pieces of silver. When the child is born, pay her, and let her return to her own country. Long enough you have played. Now resume your duties. Hear the Command! Marry the one chosen for you. The daughter of Li becomes impatient at this long delay. The family of Li have been patient, preferring to allow the marriage to wait until your madness—known throughout the city, so that it is a scandal and a disgrace to the clan—is past. But now they will wait no longer; they demand their rights. The marriage can no longer be postponed. Youth is passing, and the sons begot and borne in youth are best."

And he handed to my brother a heavy bag of silver.

But my brother took the silver and threw it upon

[263]

the ground. He bent forward, and his eyes were like double-edged knives, seeking the other's heart. His anger had been mounting under his icy face, and now it burst forth as terrible as lightning unforeseen out of a clear sky.

"Return to that one!" he shouted. "Bid him take back his silver! From this day I have no father. I have no clan—I repudiate the name of Yang! Remove my name from the books! I and my wife, we will go forth. In this day we shall be free as the young of other countries are free. We will start a new race—free—free from these ancient and wicked bondages over our souls!"

And he strode out of the room.

The messenger picked up the purse muttering,

"Ah, there are other sons—there are other sons!"

And he returned to my father.

Ah, My Sister, do you see now why I said it was well that my mother died? How could she have endured to see this day? How could she have endured to see the son of a concubine take the place of her only son, the heir?

My brother has nothing now, therefore, of the

family estates. With his share they will placate the house of Li for the outrage done them, and already, Wang Da Ma says, they are looking for another husband for that one who was my brother's betrothed.

With what a sacrifice of love has my brother loved this foreigner!

But he has told her nothing of the sacrifice, her, the expectant one, lest it darken her happiness in the future. He said only,

"Let us leave this place now, my heart. There can never be a home for us within these walls."

And she was glad and went with him joyfully. Thus did my brother leave forever his ancestral home. There was not even one to bid him farewell, except old Wang Da Ma, who came and wept and bowed her head into the dust before him, crying,

"How can the son of my mistress leave these courts? It is time that I died—it is time that I died!"

They live now in a little two-story house like ours on the Street of the Bridges. My brother within this

[265]

short time has grown older and more quiet. For the first time in his life he has to think where food and clothes must come from. He goes every day early in the morning to teach in the government school here, he who never rose in the morning until the sun was swinging high in the heavens. His eyes are resolute, and he speaks less often and smiles less easily than he used. I ventured to say to him one day,

"Do you regret anything, my brother?"

He flashed one of his old quick looks at me from under his eyelids, and he replied,

"Never!"

Ah, I think my mother was wrong! He is not the son of his father. He is wholly the son of his mother for steadfastness.

Now what do you think has happened, My Sister? I laughed when I heard of it, and suddenly without understanding it I wept.

Last night my brother heard a mighty knocking on the door of his little house. He went to open it himself, since they keep but one servant in these

days, and to his amazement, there stood Wang Da
Ma. She came on a wheelbarrow, and with her she
brought all her possessions in a large woven bamboo
basket and a bundle tied in a blue cloth. When she
saw my brother she said with great calmness and
self-possession,

"I have come to live with my lady's son and to
serve her grandson."

My brother asked her,

"But do you not know that I am no longer accounted my mother's son?"

Wang Da Ma answered obstinately, grasping the
bundle and the basket firmly in either hand,

"Now then! Do you stand there and say that?
Did I not take you from your mother's arms into
these arms when you were scarce a foot in length
and as naked as a fish? Have you not fed from my
breasts? What you were born, that you are, and
your son is your son. Let it be as I say!"

My brother said he scarcely knew what to reply.
It is true that she has known us all our lives and is
more to us than a servant. While he hesitated she
moved her bundle and her basket into the little hall,

and grumbling and panting, for she grows old and fat now, she fumbled within herself for her purse. When she had found it she turned to quarrel mightily with the wheelbarrow man over the price of the fare, and thus she established herself as in her home.

This she has done for my mother's sake. It is absurd to notice over-much the behavior of a servant, nevertheless my brother laughs with an edge of tenderness in his laughter when he speaks of her. He is pleased that she is come and that in her arms his son will sleep and play.

This morning she came to pay her respects to me, and she was as always. One would think she had lived with my brother in this foreign house for years, although I know she is secretly astonished at many things. My brother says she pretends to notice nothing strange, although she distrusts especially the stairs, and nothing will induce her to climb them, for the first time, in the presence of others. But to-day she told me that she could not swallow the changes that have taken place in my mother's house.

She said that the fat concubine has become the

First Lady in my mother's place. It has been declared in the ancestral hall before the sacred tablets. She walks proudly about clad in red and purple, and on her fingers are many rings. She has even moved into my mother's rooms! Hearing Wang Da Ma tell of this, I know I can never go there again.

Ah, my mother!

※

He is tender to her, his wife, more tender now than ever since he has given up everything for her sake. He who has lived in ease all his life on his father's wealth has now become poor. But he has learned how to make her happy.

Yesterday when I went to see her she looked up from a page on which she was writing long twisting flowing lines. When I came into the room with my son she looked up smiling as she always does when she sees the child.

"I am writing to my mother," she said, her eyes suddenly illumined as they are when she smiles. "I can tell her everything at last. I shall tell her that I have hung yellow curtains at the windows and that there is a bowl of golden narcissus on the table. I shall tell her that to-day I have lined a little basket with pink silk for him to sleep in—silk the color of American apple-blossoms! She will see through every word and know how happy—how happy I am, at last!"

Have you ever seen a lovely valley, My Sister, gray beneath a heavy sky? Then suddenly the clouds part, and sunshine pours down, and life and color start out joyous and shouting from every point of that valley. It is so with her now. Her eyes are things alive in themselves for joy, and her voice is a continual song.

Her lips are never still. They are always curving and moving with little smiles and fragments of quick laughter. She is really very beautiful. I have always doubted her beauty before, because it was not like anything I had seen, but now I perceive it clearly. Storm and sullenness have gone from her eyes. They are blue like the sea under a bright sky.

As for my brother, now that he has done what he decided to do, he is quiet and grave and content. He is a man.

[270]

When I think that these two have left, each of them, a world for the other's sake, I am humbled before such love. The fruit of it will be a precious fruit—as marvelous as jade.

As for their child, I am moved in two ways. He will have his own world to make. Being of neither East nor West purely, he will be rejected of each, for none will understand him. But I think, if he has the strength of both his parents, he will understand both worlds, and so overcome.

But this is only as I think, when I watch my brother and his wife. I am only a woman. I must speak to my husband of it, since he is wise, and he knows without being told where the truth lies.

Ah, but this I do know! I long to behold their child. I wish him to be a brother to my son.

�֎֎֎֎֎֎֎֎֎֎֎֎֎֎֎֎֎

XXI

THE foreign one sings. Hour after hour songs bubble from her heart to her lips, and she is gay with a joy amazing. I, who have borne a son, rejoice with her, and in our common human experience we are knit together. We sew upon the clothes, little Chinese clothes. When she ponders upon what colors to choose she knits her brows above her smiling lips and she questions herself thus,

"Now if his eyes are black he will need this scarlet, but if his eyes are gray, he must have rose-pink. Will his eyes be black or gray, little sister?" She turns her laughing eyes to me.

Then I, smiling back, inquire,

"What color are they already in your heart?"

And she says, flushing and suddenly shy before me,

"They are black, always; let us take the scarlet."

"Scarlet is the color of joy," I tell her, "and it always is suitable for a son."

Together we know that we have chosen wisely.

I showed her then the tiny first clothes of my son, and together we placed the patterns upon the scarlet flowered satin and upon the soft scarlet silk. I myself have embroidered the little tiger-faced shoes. On such tasks we have grown near, each to the other. I have forgotten that she was ever strange. She has become my sister. I have learned to call her name. Mary—Mary!

When all was complete she made a little set of foreign clothes such as I had never seen for simplicity and fineness. I marveled at the gossamer cloth. The minute sleeves were set into the long, skirt-like robe with lace more fine than embroidery, and the cloth, though not silk, was as soft as mist. I asked her,

"How will you know when to clothe him in these?"

She smiled and patted my cheek swiftly. She has sweet, coaxing ways now that she is gay.

"Six days of the week he shall be his father's child, but on the seventh I shall dress him in linen and lace, and he shall be American." Then she was suddenly grave. "At first I thought I could make him wholly Chinese, but now I know that I must give him America also, for it is myself. He will belong to both sides of the world, my little sister—to you and to me both."

I smiled again at her. I see how it is that she has drawn my brother's heart out of him and holds it fast!

Now has their child come to us, My Sister! I have received him in my arms from the hands of Wang Da Ma. Murmuring and laughing with pride she gave him to me. I gazed upon him with eagerness.

He is a man child, a child of strength and vigor. It is true that he is not beautiful as my son is beautiful. A son like my husband's and mine could not be born a second time. But the son of my brother and of my sister is not like any other. He has the great bones and the lusty vigor of the West. But his hair and his eyes are black like ours, and his skin, though clear as jade, is dark. I can see already that in his eyes and about his lips is a look of my own mother. With what a mingling of pain and gladness do I see it!

Yet to my sister I did not speak of the likeness. I bore her child to her laughing. I said,

"See what thou hast done, my sister! Into this tiny knot hast thou tied two worlds!"

She lay back faint, exhausted, smiling.

"Place him here beside me," she whispered, and I did it.

He lay against her milk-white breast, dark and black-eyed. His mother rested her eyes on him. She touched his black hair with her white fingers.

"He must wear the red coat," I said, smiling at the sight. "He is far too dark for the white."

"He is like his father and I am satisfied," she said simply.

[275]

Then her husband came in and I withdrew myself.

❋

Last night after the child's birth I stood beside my husband in our son's room. Together we looked out of the open window into the moonlit night. The air was very clear, and our little garden was like a painting, brushed in black and white. The trees stood pointed against the sky, ebony tipped with the silver of the moon.

Behind us our son lay sleeping in his bamboo bed. He is growing too big for it now, and as he slept he flung out his arms, and his hands struck softly against the sides. He is a man altogether these days! We looked at each other in pride, my husband and I, as we heard his strong, sturdy breathing.

And then I thought of the little new-born child, and how already he looked like my mother, whose life went out as his began. I said softly with a faint sadness,

"With what pain of separation has the child of our brother and our sister taken on his life! The separation of his mother from her land and her race; the pain of his father's mother, giving up her only son; the pain of his father, giving up his home and his ancestors and the sacred past!"

But my husband only smiled. He put his arm about my shoulders. Then he said gravely,

"Think only of this—with what joy of union he came into the world! He has tied together the two hearts of his parents into one. Those two hearts, with all their difference in birth and rearing—differences existing centuries ago! What union!"

Thus he comforted me when I remembered past sadness. He will not allow me to cling to anything because it is old. He keeps my face set to the future. He says,

"We must let all that go, my Love! We do not want our son fettered by old, useless things!"

And thinking of these two, of my son and his cousin-brother, I know that my husband is right—always right!

COLOPHON

This is the eighth in the series of **Oriental Novels of Pearl S. Buck**. Other titles include *Dragon Seed, Imperial Woman, The Living Reed, The Mother, The Pavilion of Women, Sons,* and *Three Daughters of Madame Liang.*

The book was printed and bound by R. R. Donnelley & Sons Company, Harrisonburg, Virginia on acid free paper. The text and display type are Times New Roman.